My Brother John

**Center Point
Large Print**

**This Large Print Book carries the
Seal of Approval of N.A.V.H.**

ॐ श्री गणेशाय नमः

My Brother John

Herbert Purdum

Center Point Publishing
Thorndike, Maine

This Center Point Large Print edition
is published in the year 2002 by arrangement with
Golden West Literary Agency.

The text of this Large Print edition is unabridged. In other
aspects, this book may vary from the original edition. Printed in
Thailand. Set in 16-point Times New Roman type by
Bill Coskrey and Gary Socquet.

ISBN 1-58547-224-7

Library of Congress Cataloging-in-Publication Data.

Purdum, Herbert R.
    My brother John / Herbert Purdum.--Center Point large print ed.
    p. cm.
    ISBN 1-58547-224-7 (lib. bdg. : alk. paper)
    1. Large type books. I. Title.

PS3566.U666 M9 2002
813'.54--dc21

2002022265

FOR "BUTCH"
WITH LOVE AND GRATITUDE

I

IT WAS MY KIND of country, this upland section of the Territory. Big lonesome frontier country full of wild critters, some of which were human. Oh, there were some civilized folks but they were mostly crowded up together in scattered settlements. The rest was still raw untamed land where a man could grow full-sized and claim anything, do anything and be anything he was big enough and tough enough to back up.

My kind of country. The kind I'd headed for thirteen years ago when I decided that any male Texan who was fifteen years old and owned long pants, a hoss and a gun was too old a man to be sent off to school every morning. My folks didn't exactly agree so I rode off one day when Ma had dragged Pa to some church doings in town. I figgered they still had my kid brother, John. He liked going to school. In fact John even liked going to church, so much he wound up a preacher.

So you can see that this sure wasn't his kind of country. Not in no way, shape or form. There wasn't a church of any kind nowhere, not for a couple hundred miles anyway. No real schools neither. There wasn't hardly no roads even. Just overgrown trails like the one I was on. No, sir, it wasn't no kind of country for a man like my brother.

But as I rode Slug, my big gray gelding, towards the town called Concho, and leading a pack hoss, I was following nobody else but my brother, John.

Some five or six miles from town we pulled up to let the hosses blow. I hooked my leg around the saddle horn and rolled a cigarette while I eyed John unhappily. As brothers go I suppose John was a pretty good one. He was a few years younger than me but I didn't hold that against him. John had a likable easygoing way about him and he had plenty of brains, even if he did waste them a good deal reading books. I suppose I couldn't really blame John for becoming a preacher. He was just natcherally bent that way ever since he was a button. If he'd only have settled down in a nice little church somewhere everything would have been fine. But not him! He had to be a circuit rider. And not just anyplace! He had to pick out the wildest, toughest part of the whole blamed frontier, where the law came in calibers and God was nothing but a word used to cuss with.

"Only a few more miles to Concho, Frank."

John gave me a little smile that was almost apologetic. He knew how I felt.

My reply was mostly a grunt. "How long we staying there?"

John frowned in thought and began digging out the crumpled bits of paper his pockets were always stuffed with. Straightening them out carefully and squinting where the penciled notes had rubbed into blurs he finally said, "Let's see. There'll be two weddings . . ."

He paused and smiled to himself. "Three maybe." He checked his notes. "About six or seven christenings. Hard to tell how many funeral services but there's always a few."

John heaved an unhappy sigh and I groaned sourly.

"Never mind, John. Trying to figure your schedule just gives me a headache."

John flashed me a look, then stared off and nodded kind of tired-like. "Me, too," he said. "If I only had someone to go ahead and organize things for me I could save so much time and—"

"No," I said.

"What?" John looked at me blankly. "I only said—"

"I won't do it."

"But, Frank, I—"

"No!" I glared at John defensively. "I couldn't do it! First time some old biddy started clawing me about having the prayer meeting at her house instead of Mrs. Whosis, I'd pop her one!"

John kind of swallowed a smile and shrugged wearily. "Well, maybe you're right."

"Damm right I'm right!" I snarled, making a gesture of savage finality.

"Don't curse, Frank," said John. He turned and stared off and I knew there was more to come.

It came. After a moment without turning he said, "Sure need somebody."

I shifted defenses. "John, you know Ma made me promise her when she was dying that I'd stay close to you and protect you as best I could."

My brother winced.

"Only thing I hold against Ma," I muttered, "her making me promise a thing like that."

John gave me a dark scowl. "Frank, I'm a grown man!

I don't need protection!"

"You'd best be careful," I warned, "or some day the Lord's gonna whop you for stretching the truth so far."

"But I don't!" protested John. "I'm a minister! What would I need protecting from?"

I shrugged. "You want me to make out a list? You can get into more trouble without even trying, than a dozen hardcases could get into on purpose."

"Oh, that's ridiculous!" John threw up his hands in hopeless despair. He wasn't licked, but before he could figure a new argument we both reacted to the sound of hosses coming toward us and moving fast.

I thumbed the rawhide loop off the hammer of my .44 Colt, making sure the heavy revolver was loose in its holster. Which sounds maybe a little strange but I learned a long time ago that when you rode through country like this you didn't let nobody ride up on you without you being ready to hand out welcome or war as might be required. There were folks in the territory that didn't think it was necessary to be so careful but most of them were buried.

There were two riders, a short skinny jasper on a long-legged dun and a tall skinny one forking a fast-looking roan. The little fellow was dark and wore flashy cowboy duds, but the low-tied guns told you that Little Man's business was more than just cows. And the vicious curl on the end of his smile made it clear that this was a lad who enjoyed his work.

The beanpole wore a farmer's bib overalls and a faded blue shirt, a sweat-stained shapeless hat and one gun, an old Remington belted high around his waist for a cross-draw. At a quick glance he was just a simple clod with dull china-blue eyes, but I remembered something Pa had said about the cross-draw being a big edge when a man was on hossback. I took me another look at the beanpole and this time I noticed how his right hand rested on the saddle horn only an inch or so from the gutta-percha handle of his big Remington. My eyes went back to his face and I became aware of the hard planes under the beardstubble on his face and saw the cold glints of light flash deep in those dull blue eyes. I felt a little shiver go down my spine. The little one looked like the gunfighter, but the beanpole was the man-killer.

It was the tall one who held up his hand, palm forward in the peace sign, and gave us a smile of greeting.

"Hoddy, fellers," he drawled. "One of you happen to be the circuit rider?"

John nodded with a friendly smile and said, "I'm the Reverend Niles, sir. This is my brother, Frank."

My nod wasn't so friendly but it didn't make any difference. The two riders weren't paying me no attention at all.

"We come to get you for Colonel Belknap," said the little man.

"He wants for you to do some marryin'," said the beanpole, grinning.

I stiffened like I'd been jabbed by a Comanche lance. "That be Colonel Rye Belknap? Big He of the Saber Ranch?"

The little one didn't take his eyes off my brother but he

nodded curtly. "None other, Jack." It was the tall man who turned now and looked me over. He didn't miss a thing, neither.

John smiled. "Well, I'll be happy to perform Colonel Belknap's wedding—"

Little Man smiled sarcastically, "Figgered you would, Preach. He's in a hurry, so let's ramble."

"What?" John looked startled. "Oh, I'm sorry, I didn't mean—that is, I can't possibly do it today. But as soon as I've taken care of my obligations to the people of Concho—"

Little Man shook his head. "You don't seem to hear very good, Preach. Does he, Scanlan?"

The beanpole's gaze left me reluctantly and he smiled at John. His voice was soft as a falling snowflake. As cold, too.

"He just don't understand, Cory. Better explain that when Colonel Belknap wants a man to do something, he does it."

"You see, Preach," began Cory, "when Colonel Bel—"

"I heard him!" said John, anger staining his cheeks. "But I simply can't—"

"Easy way or hard way," Scanlan purred, "he does it."

I I

I SAW JOHN'S hands swiftly double into fists but before he could say anything more the little gunman, Cory, chuckled wickedly, "Me, I kinda like when it's the hard way, Preach. Gives a man a chance to get some exercise."

With the words his right hand blurred downward, came up holding a gun. He gigged his hoss and stood in his stirrups to swing the long-barreled revolver in a vicious cut at John's head.

The blow never came close to connecting. I drew my gun with the smooth, almost lazy-seeming motion that Pa had drilled into me and leveled it across the saddle horn. Yelling for John to duck I thumbed the hammer and saw the little gunhawk smashed out of the saddle by the heavy slug. He hit the ground with a screech. I covered him all the way with the hammer ready to drop again but it wasn't necessary. Little Man had given up all thoughts of gunplay, clutching his bloody shoulder and moaning pitifully.

But while I was boring Cory the beanpole nearly coiled my twine for good. I caught the blur of movement as he made his cross-draw, but even as I swung my gun to bear on him I knew I was gonna be too late.

Then my brother went out of his saddle after Scanlan like a bobcat springing on a rabbit. The beanpole's Remington boomed but the bullet went wild because the tall gunman was on his way to the ground with John all over him. When they landed it broke John's grip enough for Scanlan to tear loose from him. The gunman came to his knees and brought up his gun to blast John's head off but by then I had the gray in motion and leaning over I smashed my gun barrel against Scanlan's skull, driving him face down into the dirt.

From the way the beanpole's body went lax I knew he was out of it. If he wasn't dead he'd at least have the grandaddy of all headaches when he came to.

I pulled Slug around and swung down. John was getting up and brushing the dirt from his coat, giving me a grateful smile. In return I scowled at him angrily, being still on edge, not that my disposition has ever been the sweetest or my temper the best-controlled.

"Don't you know any better than to jump on a man holding a cocked revolver?" I blared at him.

"Yes," admitted John meekly. "But I had to, Frank. If I hadn't, you wouldn't have been able to save my life."

I started to nod, then stopped and flushed as I got his meaning. John smiled at me and turned to start digging in his saddlebags.

Not coming up with any answers that would sound even a little bit sensible I turned away sulkily and saw the little gunman still sitting and clutching his bullet-smashed shoulder, rocking in pain. I eyed him savagely and took a couple of steps towards him, lifting my gun. He looked up and uttered a piteous wail, then from behind me came my brother's sharp voice:

"Frank, no!"

John came around me with bandages and carbolic for the man's wound, looking at me in shocked disapproval. I looked it right back at him.

"You mean you ain't gonna let me finish off these two snakes?"

John just gave me one of his Looks. I don't know exactly how to describe it but John's Look was something I'd never found a way to beat or even argue against. Knowing this made me so mad I could have strangled him sometimes, and this was one of the times. But getting mad didn't do no good, nothing did.

John had swiped the trick from Ma. She was a wonderful person but there were times when I was a kid when she drove me nuts. She not only was smart enough to stay two jumps ahead of John and me—mostly me—but there was times when I was sure she had fourteen eyes, including some in the back of her head. Like in church. I usually managed to sit pretty far away and behind her. For all the good it did I might as well have sat in her lap. Because the first move I made to sneak out a rubber band or some spitballs I'd hear Ma's fingers snapping. Snap! Snap! It wasn't loud but that sound was a message I didn't dare ignore. I still jumped when I heard somebody snap their fingers twice like that. It was Ma's command to look at her, and you can bet I did, even when I was scared to. Of course when I did, I got the Look, and that stopped whatever I was doing wrong, and quick. Didn't matter if I thought what I was doing was all right, didn't matter if I felt mean and defiant, when I got the Look I just froze up, feeling helpless and guilty.

John's Look had the same effect on me. It stopped me cold. Oh, I tried hard enough to fight my way past it but I didn't have a chance and knowing that made me boil over with wicked fury.

I guess the little gunman, Cory, didn't realize John had me buffaloed and that I was mad mostly at myself. He took one look at my face and cringed back, bleating, "No, you can't! That would be murder!"

I snarled, "What the hell do you think it's gonna be if we turn you two loose to talk to Belknap?"

John glanced up from his work on Cory's shoulder.

"Don't curse, Frank."

"Who's cussing? I only said hell—"

"Frank."

"Well, for the luvva Pete," I strangled, "hell ain't cussing! You say it yourself! And in *church!*"

All that earned me was another Look. I shifted back to the matter of leaving the two gunmen alive to carry tales to Belknap. John kept shaking his head and going on with his bandaging.

"No," he said firmly. "No, I know Colonel Belknap has a bad reputation, Frank, but even he wouldn't—"

"He would and he has, John! Belknap's made his brag all over the territory that nobody crosses him or his Saber outfit. Not and lives to talk about it!"

My brother's face settled into stubborn lines. He said in a quiet tone, "Frank, why argue about it? You're not going to kill these two men and you know it. I don't think you could even if I agreed with you."

"Try me," I begged. John ignored my plea to finish the bandaging. I picked up Cory's guns, lifted Scanlan's, and threw them far off into the brush, stomping around in bitter frustration.

"All right. All right, John," I finally muttered. "I don't suppose it matters a hell—a heck of a lot. Riding with you I got no chance for a long life anyway."

I picked up Slug's reins and the ugly brute promptly tried for my arm, his teeth clashing in a whisker-thin miss. He snorted in angry frustration, keeping an evil red eye open for another opportunity as I swung up into the saddle. Daydreaming around Slug was about as safe as playing patty-cake with a starving grizzly bear, and I knew I'd better remember it or some day I'd be pulling back a nub.

John was looking at the unconscious Scanlan and the wounded Cory unhappily and now looked at me.

"It's not very humane to just leave them here," he began; then at the look on my face he stopped, sighed, shook his head a little and mounted, adding, "but I suppose it's all we can do."

I made some kind of noise. It must have sounded pretty awful the way John turned to look at me, but I didn't care, I still figured it was crazy to leave them in condition to report to Colonel Belknap. From what I'd heard, he'd be about as forgiving as a stepped-on rattlesnake.

As usual my brother sensed what I was thinking and flashed me a consoling smile.

"Faith, brother," he said.

He started his hoss and in a moment he broke out singing a Negro spiritual.

> Now I tole de Lawd I'se a sinner man,
> As bad as I could be:
> But de good Lawd said, Jest foller me,
> An' I will set yu free!
>
> Yes, de good Lawd said, jest foller me,
> An' I will set yu free! . . .

John's voice was deep and mellow and most times I

kinda liked listening to him sing, but right now it didn't seem to help. Just then Slug arched his back and tried a quick pitch. I balled up one horny fist and walloped him between the ears so hard his knees buckled. For a moment Slug stood there shaking his head and snorting indignantly, then he shook himself a little and started after John, prancing for all the world like he'd been told what a good boy he was. That was my Slug. Treat him sweet and gentle and he'd do his best to kick your head off and act sulky all day if he missed. Belt him one and he turned into Mama's Little Lamb and would run his ugly heart out for you.

Slug really should have been a mare.

I I I

MOST FOLKS would figure it was tough enough trying to stay alive on the frontier, what with red Injuns and wild critters and just plain badmen running around loose and looking for trouble, without deliberately taking on a killer outfit like Saber. Leastway I've only known one man who was reasonably sane that had that kind of nerve—only he called it faith.

My brother, John.

Now I've always held that it was every man's good old U.S. American right to get himself killed any way he happened to like, and I ain't gonna back down on that. If John was risking just his own neck I wouldn't buck at all, but Ma having stuck me with the job of being his protector meant that my neck was out too, and that was a hoss of nine different colors.

Not that it made a nickel's worth of difference to John. First off he didn't think he needed protecting—which is why he did, of course. Then second, he'd do whatever he figured was right no matter what. He'd have himself a little powwow with the Man Upstairs to get His okay, then wade right in, happy as two fleas on a shaggy dog. The whole problem was that John wasn't happy just preaching religion. He had to live it. Not only on Sunday, but every day in the week.

There you are.

Now don't go getting me wrong. I ain't got a thing against religion. Fact is I always felt a little religion was good for a fellow. I've gone to church plenty of times, and before I joined up with John, too. So you can see that I ain't got nothing against religion. Or preachers.

No, nor against my brother, neither—except the way he got his neck bowed about certain things, like not letting me finish off those two Saber gunhawks. And if it meant that Colonel Belknap and his crew of warriors would soon be on his tail roaring for blood John would get all the more stubborn. He was plain hell on things he called principles, John was. If it was a principle he'd stick and you couldn't talk him off it or knock him off it or buy him off it or drag him off it!

All of which wouldn't have mattered a hoot to me, except that when Saber came roaring up on his tail, mine was gonna be twitching right next to his.

So I was getting some depressed and out of sorts by the time we rode into sight of Concho. It wasn't much of a town. One main street that wabbled and drifted off slaunchwise at the far end, maybe four blocks long altogether, with two or three cross streets that didn't go no place. Mostly warped frame buildings with false fronts. All put together it wasn't nothing to lift a man's spirits none.

When we neared the edge of town a sturdy brown eight-year-old boy popped out of some bushes riding a broomhandle pony and leveling a wooden pistol at us.

"Powww!" he yelled. "Powww! Powww! Yu're daid, yu redskins! Bite the dust! Powww!"

It wasn't no time nor place to jump out at me waving even a wooden pistol. I guess I must have reacted kinda sudden for the kid skidded to a halt and turned as white as he could with six jillion freckles on his map.

"Jim Maginnis! Hi, Jim," John called out, then saw how the kid was staring popeyed and frozen in my direction and jerked around in the saddle to see why. I let down the hammer and got the gun back in my holster as quick as I could and gave John a feeble smile.

"He kinda startled me, John."

John snorted in disgust and turned back to the boy, who now gulped a couple of times then turned on a gap-toothed grin that busted my heart in a thousand pieces. For a kid like that I'd almost be willing to commit matrimony with a woman.

John and the boy exchanged greetings and then John waved at me and said I was his brother, Frank. The boy turned to me a little hesitantly so I smiled wryly and said, "It's all right, boy. I only bite on Tuesdays. Didn't mean to throw down on you."

The boy looked at me gravely, then nodded. "Yu cain't he'p it. Some fellers air jest more skeery than others."

He looked back at John worshipfully, adding, "But yu got Rev'rend John to take keer of yu. I gotta go now, I gotta tell everybody the circuit rider's come!"

The kid spun his broom-handle mount and legged it into town, hollering the news while I was still strangling over his comments. That little d—! Well, I'd sure straighten him out the next time I saw him. It didn't help none to have John grinning at me, either, though he did his best to blank his face.

If my mood had been sour before it had turned downright spoiled now. I would have almost been happy to have seen Saber riding up so I could at least shoot somebody. I was feeling about as sorry for myself as a man could without busting out crying.

Ahead of me my brother, John, started to sing again. You see?

Finally John glanced over his shoulder and with a frown he dropped back alongside of me.

"Something wrong, Frank?" he asked worriedly.

"Something . . ." I threw up my hands and groaned hopelessly. "For the love of mud, you forgot! I swear you don't even remember!"

"Remember what?" John looked perplexed. "Oh . . . you mean what happened with those two riders from Saber?"

I took a long deep breath, then said grimly, "John, a couple of months ago Belknap's men strung up a cowboy by his thumbs—"

John reacted in horror. "By his thumbs!"

"You know why? Because he was caught riding across Saber land. That's all he did! Now, do you have any idea what they'll do to us?"

John looked at me soberly. "Is that story true, Frank?"

"It's true. But it ain't the worst or anywhere near the worst thing Belknap's done."

John's face settled into hard lines and he shook his head. "Something," he said quietly, "should be done about a man like that."

For a minute I couldn't get my breath. I just choked and gurgled at that incredible brother of mine. I finally managed to wheeze, "Wait, wait, we ain't the U.S. Cavalry, John. Belknap's got forty-fifty riders on the Saber payroll. Meanest bunch of gunslicks in the Territory!"

John didn't even seem to hear me. "It's not right," he brooded, "for a man to misuse such power. If a man keeps using such power for wickedness, then the power should be taken away from him."

"Taken away fr—" I gasped, then swallowed hard a couple of times and said hastily, "Uh . . . look, I know how you hate shooting and killing, John, so why don't we grab some fresh hosses and line out for Fort Dixon? It's only a hundred miles or so. With any luck we—"

"Fort Dixon?" asked John puzzledly. "But why on earth would we want to go there?"

I wanted to sit down and bawl. What was the use? I shrugged and waved my hand in complete defeat.

"Aw, I dunno," I muttered. "Never mind. I lost my head."

John's face suddenly crinkled in a smile of deep affection and he reached over and put his hand on my shoulder.

"I know, Frank. I know you're only thinking of my safety. But even if I wanted to run I couldn't. I have duties and obligations to the people of Concho."

"They could wait."

"No," said John with a firm headshake, "after they've waited six months for me that's long enough."

John gave my shoulder a squeeze and smiled. "Come on, Frank, enough gloominess. Colonel Belknap will probably forget the whole thing."

By now a dozen people were heading for us with excited waves and lighted faces of welcome, calling John's name. Traveling around with John on his circuit had made me aware of how important the circuit rider was to these people on the frontier. And it wasn't just the sermons he preached, and it wasn't just the marryings and buryings and christenings and such, either. He was a combination of Solomon and Mister Fixit between folks that came to loggerheads over something or other. Be it a husband-and-wife argument over who's gonna wear the britches in the family, or whether Jump-up Jones had the right to carve on the gizzard of a drummer who cheated at cribbage, it was John who had to settle it. He was the onliest man all sides of an argument would trust for a fair and square decision.

Which was just one of the reasons why I had the life expectancy of a tissue-paper cat in hell! Because no matter how fair and square the decision was, some losers always got sore afterwards and figured maybe John was a little too fair and square, or maybe changed their mind and wanted an un-square decision, and sometimes they tried to push John around to their side of the beef.

As likely you've noticed, John, he don't push for sour owl crap, so things had a way of getting pretty smokey, and when the caps started busting, guess who'd be right in the middle gettin' himself chewed up, knocked down and tromped on? Uh-huh, none other.

One thing for sure and certain though, it did keep life from ever getting dull.

I V

ABOUT FOUR OR five hours later I was sitting against the wall in Steiner's General Store with my feet propped up on the pickle barrel trying to figure what we were going to do if Colonel Belknap and a dozen gunhawks steamed into town looking for the circuit rider and his big brother. I'd considered and thrown out four possible plans when somebody streaked by outside, riding like seventeen devils were on his tail. Only by the look I had through the fly-specked window it was *her* tail, a willow-slim girl in men's britches and shirt with a long thick rope of dark red hair flying level in the wind. I couldn't tell what her face looked like, but I had some mighty strong opinions about girls that wore men's pants, so I just grunted and went back to my figuring.

I was working on plan number seven and not liking it any better than the first six when two more riders went roaring down the street outside. This time I took a good look and felt that old familiar chunk of ice start formin' in my stomach. The first rider was a monstrous hunk of man I'd never seen before, but the second one was the over-alled beanpole, Scanlan, with a bandage tied around his head where I'd walloped him with my gun barrel.

I waited for the rest of Saber's army to show up, but that was all, just the two of them. And the way they scooted past, it didn't figure they were looking for me and John nohow. Which was a puzzle I couldn't make head nor tail of.

John was there in the store talking to the owner, a chubby little fellow named Ben Steiner, and a big raw-boned leather-skinned woman with the unlikely name of Effie Peach. Effie was the town's blacksmith, having took over when her husband was killed by Comanches a few years back. She looked like a blacksmith in her leather apron and man's shirt with the sleeves rolled up. Some said she was a better blacksmith than her husband had ever been. I didn't doubt it a bit. She had a tough look and her voice sounded like a load of rocks being dumped down a tin chute.

When I turned to talk to John, Effie was saying, "Then after the services I thought I'd serve some refreshments. Oh, just something light. Some sandwiches and pies, maybe some cake and coffee. And maybe a few pieces of chicken and—"

The plump little storekeeper groaned and held his stomach.

"Something light! Did you hear the woman?"

Effie grinned at him and said, "Wrestling the devil's

hard work. Can't do it on tea and crackers."

I winced as she walloped Steiner on the back with a anvil-sized hand and guffawed, "Not even a sweet little feller like you, Benjamin!"

Steiner was staggered by the wallop, but he recovered and glared at her, drawing himself up to his full five feet four inches.

"No," he snarled bitterly, "you just knocked the sweetness out of me. Along with dislocating my collarbone."

He gingerly rubbed the injured spot, and Effie looked at him in quick alarm. She started to reach for him.

"Aw, now I only—"

The chubby storekeeper jerked away from her, yapping, "Keep those bone crushers off me, or I'll bite!"

Effie blinked a couple of times and looked like she wanted to bawl, then suddenly turned it into a scowl.

"Why, you tender little pipsqueak! I—"

"Stop it, you two!" John looked up from jotting a note on a scrap of paper, stuffed it into his pocket. "Tuesday's full, now for Wednesday, I'll be doing the funeral services for Paul Richie, for the Owens' boy—"

"And Tom Maginnis," said Steiner.

John looked shocked. "No, not—but how?"

Steiner shrugged. "Stampede accident."

"Accident my foot!" snapped Effie. "Cold-blooded murder it was! Belknap couldn't marry a woman who had a husband, so he arranged for her to become a widow—"

"Close your mouth, Effie!" Ben Steiner's round face was set in disapproving lines. "There's no proof of that."

Effie sniffed scornfully. Before she could reply to the

little storekeeper I called to John, "Speaking of murder, John, two Saber hands just rode into town."

As I could have guessed, John merely looked puzzled. "Now, Frank, they probably came in for supplies. After all, this is the only town for fifty miles—"

"Saber must be starving them," I said. "Those two riders were nearly killing their hosses."

John smiled at me. "I'm sure there's a simple explanation."

I gave him back the smile. "One of them was the beanpole I cracked over the head. The one called Scanlan."

I finally got a reaction. Not just from John, but from the storekeeper and the woman as well.

"Oh." That was John's reaction, but Steiner turned four shades lighter and gurgled, "S-scanlan? Lou Scanlan?"

"Why he's one of Belknap's worst killers!" gasped Effie. "If you hit him, you've got to get out of here! Saber'll stake you both out over anthills!"

I shook my head and propped my feet back up on the pickle barrel. "Tell John. I'm already scared."

John chuckled. "Frank doesn't know the meaning of the word *fear.*"

"The hell—heck I don't!" I shouted. "I—"

Just about then the door exploded open and the freckle-faced kid we'd met that morning came busting in, heading for Steiner like a locoed maverick. Coming to where my legs were blocking the way he didn't slow a bit, just bent over and kept going, only he straightened up a little soon. Which didn't bother him, but it tipped my feet up just enough and sent me over on my head in a tangle of me, the chair, a small open keg of ax handles and a couple of stacks of tin washbasins.

Jim Maginnis skidded to a halt in front of Steiner.

"MisterSteinercanIhavesomecredit?"

The storekeeper chuckled, "Whoa, whoa, boy, slow down."

The boy took a deep breath. "I said . . . can I have some credit?"

Steiner blinked.

"Well, now. Credit, eh?" he said thoughtfully.

"I'll vouch for Jim," said Effie.

"So will I," said John.

Steiner scratched his head and nodded slowly. "Pretty good references. I suppose in that case I could advance you a nickel's worth of candy—"

During this Jim was nearly hopping up and down In his frantic impatience. Now he said, "No, no, no, no, sir, yu don't understand! I don't want candy! I gotta have a gun and some bullets!"

"Gun?" gasped Steiner, exchanging looks with John and Effie.

"Yessir, please, hurry!" replied the boy pleadingly. "They're hurtin' Mom and I gotta shoot 'em!"

Effie gasped, "They're doin' what?"

John hunkered down to face the boy on his own level and said to him quietly, "Who's hurting your Mom, Jim?"

"Those two men, they're tryin' to make her go with them!"

I came up in time to ask, "Where are they, Jim?"

The boy looked at me quickly. "Down in front of the

livery stable. One of 'em's a real big man, and the other's—"

"Never mind, I know who he is," I said.

John straightened up, pressing the boy over to Effie, who squatted and threw an arm around his shoulders.

"You stay here with Mrs. Peach," John told the boy. "I'll take care of this."

"We," I said.

John nodded and we headed for the front door. Jim started after us but Effie's big fist collared the boy and held him back.

"Be careful, Rev'rend John!" yelled the boy. "They got guns!"

V

OUTSIDE WE MADE tracks down the boardwalk. John glanced at me, then at my gun, then said, "No gunplay unless it's absolutely necessary, Frank."

"If it is you're undressed," I snapped sourly. "What are you going to do, throw rocks?"

John heaved a sigh. "I'm a man of peace, Frank." He sighed again. "I wish you'd understand that."

Before I could answer we reached the corner; turning it, we saw something that sent us into a dead run. In front of the livery stable Scanlan was manhandling the girl with the mop of red hair. She couldn't have been much over five feet. She barely came to the beanpole's shoulder, but she was fighting him with all the fury of a starving weasel, which there ain't nothing that can match for no-holds-barred scrapping. She was stomping on Scanlan's feet, kicking his shins, jabbing her elbows in his ribs, slapping and clawing at his eyes with her one free hand, and when we got close, we could see that the Saber gunman was looking about as miserable as a man could get, trying to hang on to her.

With her free hand the girl snatched up a piece of wood, broke it over his skull with a whap that made me wince, tried and missed with a broken horseshoe, tried again and connected so hard it bounced out of her hand.

"Stop it, aw will you stop it?" Scanlan wailed. He turned his head and hollered, "Fer Gawd's sake, Brian, hurry it up!"

Turning his head was a mistake, for the girl grabbed up a hunk of rock big enough to bash his eyebrows down around his knees. But just then John yelled:

"Turn loose of her, Mister!"

Scanlan spun around so quick in surprise that he lost hold of the girl's other hand, and she promptly used both to lift the rock over her head, plainly meaning to stop his clock for keeps.

John yelped, "No, no, don't, Mrs. Maginnis!"

The girl looked at him, the rock still held to strike. "Why not?" she asked puzzledly.

Scanlan saw the rock now and leaped frantically to one side, coming down in a crouch and glaring at us like a poisoned pup.

"Yu again! Yu two . . ." He choked on his fury, practically frothing at the mouth. Then his hand flashed to his gun, and I gave John a shove that sent him sprawling, at the same time scooping my gun out of leather. There wasn't no need for me doing either one. Scanlan had forgotten the girl.

When she saw him reach for his gun she snapped, "Stop that!" Then at a distance of five feet she chunked that rock as hard as she could. It met Scanlan's battered head with a sound like a watermelon busting, and the beanpole crumpled up like a pair of pants with the man taken out.

The girl suddenly looked at John in apology. "Oh, I'm sorry, Reverend Niles."

John rose and gave her a warm smile. "I'm grateful."

As I picked up Scanlan's gun, I was suddenly struck by something and looked at the girl, who was looking at John like he'd just saved her from a fate worse than death, like they say in them the-ayter handbills.

"Hey!" I said in surprise. "How come you didn't scream or something?"

She turned her head and looked at me blankly.

"Scream? I was mad, not scared."

With that she turned back to John, only then she noticed her shirt was torn, her shirttails pulled out and various other damage. Now this pint-sized girl had just downed a tough gunman with no help from us, but all of a sudden she turned flustery and female.

"Oh! Oh, dear!" she gasped. "Look at me, I'm a wreck! Wait right here, I'll be right back! I'll run over to Maggie's and put myself together."

She was halfway across the street by the time she finished speaking, running like a shot-at deer. Watching her run I lost a good-sized piece of my prejudice against women wearing men's clothes. In fact I lost doggone near all of it as far as that particular girl was concerned. She might be slim, and she sure wasn't no taller'n a minnit, but let me tell you it didn't take but one look to know she was a full-growed woman with all the required geography in all the right places.

I shook my head kind of dizzy-like and muttered, "Now, that's a woman!"

John gave me a quick look. "Yes," he murmured, "that's what she seems to be all right."

I opened my mouth to singe him for that crack, but a bull started bellering loud enough to lift the neck hair on a dead Comanche.

"Here now!" it roared. "What in the name of seven green hoptoads is goin' on out here?"

Coming out of the stable leading a saddled horse was the monster I'd seen riding into town with Scanlan. Six and a half feet and two hundred and fifty pounds of the toughest-looking black Irishman I ever want to lay eyes on. His sleeves were rolled to his elbows and in his waistband was stuck an enormous old Walker Colt conversion. Scowling darkly, he ignored John and me and stalked over to where Scanlan was starting to stir. He made no offer to help the beanpole, just stood over him with his huge mallet fists on his hips. Scanlan slowly pushed to a sitting position.

"Well, Scanlan?" rumbled the giant acidly. "Are ye too tired to stand up like a man? And would ye be tellin' me now, why ye let the girl run off?"

"Let her!" Scanlan groaned and held his head. "Aw, go

way, Brian, lemme alone."

Brian nodded scornfully. "Ye better go back to the ranch, 'twill be aisier to do this job by meself."

He stalked off, heading after the girl, but in two steps he found John blocking his path grimly. I lifted Scanlan's gun, keeping both Saber men covered. The monster stopped and stared at John in disbelief.

"No," said John.

Brian looked unable to believe his ears or his eyes. He shook his head a little. "Ye said—"

"The word was no," John repeated flatly. "Meaning you're to leave the lady alone."

Brian waved for John to move out of his way. "Be movin' aside like a good boy, so I won't have to be breakin' ye up into little pieces."

John shook his head stubbornly. "I'm sorry, Mister."

The Irisher looked at him gravely.

"No, ye're not sorry yet, but ye will be."

For a man so big Brian moved like a panther, swinging his great knobby fists. John was forced to drift back quickly, covering up, swaying his head so the punches whistled past, missing by a whisker and throwing the giant off balance. John stepped in and planted four straight hooks to Brian's whiskery jaws, hitting with all the power he had. But the big man only grunted, and shook his head a little, then glared at John in outrage.

"Why ye little pipsqueak! Those hurt!" Brian bellowed furiously. "I'll murder ye for that!"

The big Irisher lowered his head and charged John, his fists flailing. John locked his hands together and sidestepping the charge John powered a two-handed chop behind Brian's ear that near tore his head off and sent him sprawling, his nose plowing a furrow in the soft compost of dirt and manure that made up the stable yard.

I moved to lean against a post, rolled a smoke but kept an eye on Scanlan. I wasn't surprised at John's ability in a fight. Our pa had taught us for years, and he was the best there was with fists, boots, guns or knives. John and I didn't have no choice, Pa made us fight. He believed in it, felt that a man who couldn't hold his own in a scrap had no right wearing a man's britches. So if John and I didn't want to fight or maybe didn't feel like it, the old man would wallop us till we did, then go on to knock the stuffing out of us so we'd remember next time. By the time he was sixteen John was a match for Pa, which took some man-sized doing no matter if Pa was over forty then. I came home for a visit the year John was eighteen, and we had our last fight. I'd managed to lick him, but I was a cripple for two weeks afterwards. So even if the big Irishman did have six inches and sixty pounds of John, I didn't figger he'd take John very easy.

So I leaned against the post and smoked and enjoyed the fight. It was a lulu.

After Brian had gotten to his hands and knees, shaken his head and blown the dirt from his nose, he surged to his feet. Or started to. John wasn't about to let the monster get up and get set again. Using that same wicked two-hand chop John took good aim and clobbered the Irisher's iron jaw just as he was straightening up, and sent him spinning right back into the dirt again. When Brian rose again John was there to belt him again, the big fellow falling so hard the ground shook under my boots. About the third time John put him on the ground I was afraid it might not be much of a fight after all. But that was when Scanlan made another mistake.

As he got his senses back the gunman looked around sneaky-like for his Remington. He finally saw it spinning around on my finger, and I gave him a sweet little smile. Scanlan scowled and got to his feet shakily, so mad and frustrated I guess he didn't care if I shot him or not. Anyways he suddenly spun and jumped on John's back while John was waiting for Brian to straighten up for the fourth time.

Like I said, it was Scanlan's mistake. John went down in a rolling fall that broke Scanlan's hold. They both jumped up and Scanlan swung at John's chin with all he had. John stepped inside the roundhouse blow and punched the beanpole silly with six smacking hooks, stepping back then to let Scanlan drop on his face, back in dreamland again.

John turned on Brian just in time to meet one of the monster's fists with his jaw. It lifted John off his feet and he went crashing down on his back. Brian was still woozy but he lurched after John, aiming to finish the fight in a hurry now.

John rolled, dodging him, rolled again, getting some of the cobwebs out of his skull, then came to his hands and knees. Brian got set to powder him when he tried to straighten up, but for a preacher John could be trickier than a Pawnee hoss thief. Instead of straightening up he just hurled himself right at Brian headfirst, butting him just above the belt buckle. With an awful groan the monster staggered back, tripped over Scanlan and went sprawling on his back.

It woke Scanlan up, which was too bad for him, for he tried to jump on John's back again. This time John saw him coming and used one of them wonderful mean wrestling tricks Pa taught us. He grabbed one of the beanpole's wrists and half-turned and bent over, yanking Scanlan up and over him in a flying mare. Scanlan hit the stable wall so hard I almost expected to see him crash right through the planks. He didn't, but watching him slide down in a boneless heap it was plain that Mr. Scanlan was all through for that day. I almost felt sorry for him.

When John turned and met Brian again it was a question as to which one was the most wobble-legged. They stood toe-to-toe and slugged till Brian finally managed to half-knock, half-push John to his knees. As Brian moved in John came up again, with that wild head-butt to the pit of the Irisher's stomach, and as Brian wobbled backwards gasping for air, John went after him. Then, gathering every bit of strength he had left, John connected with the monster's jaw so hard it was a wonder Brian's head didn't go flying right off his shoulders. But all that happened was he staggered back a couple of steps, gave kind of a tired sigh, then dropped to his knees, then real slow just keeled over on his battered mug out cold.

John had to grab hold of a corral post to keep from falling himself. I was so proud of him I could of bust. I stuck Scanlan's gun in my waistband and clapped my hands. John didn't care much for my applause. He lifted his head wearily and glared at me as I came up, or that is he did the best job of glaring he could with one eye swollen shut and the other all puffy and bloodshot.

"You," he choked thickly. "You—were a lot of help, you—"

I gave him a surprised and hurt look. "But, John!" I said in injured protest. "I didn't want to interfere with such a man of peace."

V I

FOR A SECOND I thought John was gonna slug me, but then he figured it was too much trouble and giving me another one-eyed glare he turned and stalked off. I trotted after him, feeling kind of contented deep inside. It wasn't too often I came out on top with my brother so I was enjoying this one to the fullest.

It was a good thing I did. I sure didn't get to enjoy it very long. Then Mrs. Maginnis came running back across the street.

She'd fixed herself up like she said. Her mahogany-colored hair was combed and tied with a bit of green ribbon. Her face was scrubbed pink and shining. And she'd put on a dress.

Maybe that don't sound like much but it was more than enough for me. It was a frilly green dress cinched up tight around her middle with a sort of a scooped-out neckline that was low enough to give me a fever at thirty paces and for sure rid me of any doubts about her being a full-grown-type woman. And her—but no, I better stop before I really get bogged down in mush.

Let me just say this: that doll-sized woman grabbed my heart and locked it up in her own private corral for good and always and permanent right then and there. And without doing a thing, not even giving me so much as a sweet look.

She couldn't. She had eyes for nothing and nobody but my brother, John. Why, the way she looked at him he was a blamed hero or something. That and maybe a martyr all rolled up into one.

"What a punch!" she cried excitedly. "What a magnificent punch! You licked Brian O'Brian!"

John gave her a feeble smile. "I don't feel like it."

Oh, the dirty dog! Naturally that made her notice his bruises and the way his clothes were torn. I guess he did look kind of beat-up. Then with him smiling so pitiful and acting so brave in spite of all the awful pain, why she just melted in sympathy of course. It was enough to make a man sick at his stomach.

"Oh, you must be feeling terrible," she gasped and moved up alongside him, taking his arm and putting it around her shoulders.

"Here, put your arm around my neck. Now, lean on me. We'll go to my house where I can put some arnica on those dreadful bruises."

John obeyed her with another brave little smile that nearly choked me. I hurried to catch up, lifting a hand in protest.

"Wait," I said. "He doesn't have to put his arm around y— I mean he can lean on me."

I grabbed John's other arm and tried to take over his weight, but John shook his head.

"I'm doing fine, Frank."

"But you're too heavy for her."

She glanced at me coldly. "He's not leaning hard."

I swallowed helplessly and tried to think of another approach. Like a tongue-tied fool all I could do was mumble. I finally blurted, "I'm his brother."

She looked at me without expression. "Are you?"

I swallowed again. "My name's Frank."

She didn't say anything to that so after a pause I said, "I'm not a preacher though."

She still didn't say anything.

"I—I just travel around with him," I stammered, "to kind of look after him and—"

I stopped suddenly, feeling a little sick.

She looked at me, then looked at John.

"He's joshing," she said.

I groaned, "Aw, you don't understand. It was only . . . that is, I would have . . . well, I knew he could . . ."

I stopped, knowing I couldn't explain it so it made any sense. Scowling darkly I muttered, "Never mind."

I dropped back behind them feeling suddenly old and futile. It didn't perk me up none to hear John's comment, neither.

"Too much sun I guess," he murmured to her with a shake of his head.

For the first time I began to understand how Cain felt

about Abel.

Mrs. Maginnis had rented a small unpainted cottage on the outskirts of town. I trailed forlornly after her and John like an unwanted puppy. Which was about how I felt, too, what with her fussing over him and making all kind of sympathetic noises about John's injuries and generally acting like a fool female. Of course John was limping and choking back groans every few steps, acting so brave it was plain sickening. For all the attention she paid me I might as well have stayed in Steiner's store.

She did let me follow them inside the house, but when I tried to help her settle John on the sofa she sort of brushed me away like I was some kind of persistent bug or something.

"Please excuse the mess, Reverend Niles," she said to John apologetically, "I haven't finished unpacking."

"I always let my nurses call me John," said my brother with that crooked little smile of his that always made my spine crinkle and apparently had the same effect on Mrs. Maginnis only more so.

She matched his smile shyly and said, "In that case I suppose you better call me Blanche."

"Happily," John murmured.

"My name's Frank," I said to no one in particular.

Blanche paid no more attention than she had the first time I introduced myself. She fluffed up the pillows under John's head and brushed back his hair gently.

"Now you lay still, John, while I get the arnica."

With that she left the room. I shifted from one foot to the

other, looked around and found a chair. John lay peacefully content, avoiding my eyes.

I finally muttered, "You could at least put in a good word for me."

John glanced at me and nodded gravely. "I could."

He sighed and closed his one good eye, then added, "May even do it sometime. If . . . I don't forget."

"I'll remind you," I said.

"Won't help," John replied, "you know how busy I'll be making up my schedule. Of course if you were to offer to be my organizer . . ." He opened his eye to see my reaction.

"Blackmail!" I grated. He closed his eye quickly.

"Nothing of the sort. It's only—"

"Cold-blooded blackmail. Of your own brother, too!"

John said in an injured tone, "Well, if you're going to take it like that, let's forget it. I certainly wouldn't want to force you to help me."

"Not much," I sneered bitterly. "But it's not going to work."

John just heaved a sigh, keeping his eye closed. Blanche came back in then, ending it for a moment. As I watched Blanche doctoring him with iodine and liniment I tried to figure a way around John, but without much hope. I knew from too many sad experiences that outfiguring the Reverend John Niles took a lot of doing.

Besides, even bruised up, he was a handsome fellow, John was, with honest, clean-cut features, and I was unhappily aware of my own battered and scarred mug with its big nose that leaned first one way then another. It was a natcheral target, my nose, and most every fight I got into it was knocked slaunchwise again. I got into fights pretty often, not having John's good nature. Most of all I didn't have John's smile. He was mighty likable, any way you saw him; but when John smiled, his face sort of twisted and crinkled up and his eyes kinda twinkled at you, and it made you feel all warm and good inside. John could melt me at forty paces with that crooked little smile of his. He knew it too, darn him.

No matter how you figured it John was a hard man to put down. With a girl he was probably unbeatable. Which was a nice miserable bit of knowledge for me to have sitting there in Blanche Maginnis' parlor.

I had some other things on my mind just then, and I could see that John was itching with curiosity, too. We'd picked up a lot of loose pieces to a peculiar puzzle which didn't have any too nice a smell. We were involved up to our necks now. It was high time we knew what was going on with this girl and Colonel Belknap.

VII

WHEN BLANCHE finished playing nurse John asked her quietly, "Do you want to talk about it?"

Blanche kind of stiffened and half-closed her eyes but not before I saw them gleam with wicked hatred.

"No," she said slowly in reply to John. "No, I don't want to talk about it, but I guess I have to."

Neither John nor me said anything so after a moment

she went on in a low tone without emotion.

"Colonel Rye W. Belknap. Of the Virginia Belknaps. Tidewater planters for a hundred and fifty years. Real gentry. Thousands of acres of tobacco, cotton, indigo. Beautiful mansions. Wonderful horses. Oh, and slaves of course. Hundreds and hundreds of slaves. The Belknaps liked having slaves."

She paused and smiled in an ugly sort of way.

"Then their beloved Confederacy lost a war. The Belknaps were dead, all but the Colonel. The plantations were burned, the slaves freed. So he came west, determined to start a new Belknap empire, a new Belknap dynasty."

"Saber."

Blanche nodded shortly. "Saber. A few people had to die and a lot more had to run, but he built Saber into the biggest ranch in the territory. He's got his empire."

"But no empress?" I put in, beginning to see the light.

"You can't have a dynasty without sons," shrugged Blanche. "He has to have a wife who'll produce the next generation of Belknaps, or Saber dies when he does."

John was frowning at her now. "But why you, Blanche?" he asked. "A woman already married and——"

"Look around, John," exclaimed Blanche with a bitter gesture. "How many white women are there on the frontier?"

"Well, not many I know——"

"How many of them do you think would fit the Colonel's special requirements?"

She stood up and paced a little, her small fists clenched tight in remembered anger. "Oh, he even listed them for me," she went on in a metallic voice. She ticked them off on her fingers: "Beauty, intelligence, cultured, wellbred. The Colonel's very particular, you see."

"You want to hear my name for him?" I said.

John threw me a disapproving look, then said to Blanche, "And of course you fit all his requirements?"

"With a bonus," she replied acidly. "Having a son I'm proven breeding stock."

I could see John shudder at that.

"Look," he said finally, "a man of Belknap's position and wealth could go east. New York, Boston, there are many places where he could surely find—"

Blanche shook her head wearily and dropped into a chair again.

"You don't understand. That would take time. Colonel Belknap's a very impatient man. So I offered still another bonus. I'm here."

I got up impatiently. "So who needs to be offered bonuses to want a woman as beautiful as you? He's after you, that's easy to savvy. What I want to know is how come his riders were manhandling you?"

Blanche looked at me and suddenly gave me a smile. It wasn't a very big smile, but it made me stand at least two inches taller. To say nothing about the way it melted that left-out feeling I'd been feeling.

"I like to ride early in the morning," she said. "This morning Belknap's riders picked me up and took me to Saber."

"You mean—took you by force?" inquired John.

Blanche uttered a short laugh. "I certainly didn't want to

44

go! Overstreet—that's Belknap's foreman—threatened to kill Blaze, my horse, if I didn't go with them."

John shoved himself to his feet and went to stare out of the window, and I noticed that his fists were clenched tight and hard. Preacher or not, John had a man-sized temper. He was a Niles, and no Niles ever lacked that ingredient. I remember when John was a kid he used to bawl when he got really mad, and when he started bawling it was time to run. He turned into a screaming devil, and you knew he didn't just want to whup you, he wanted to tear you into little bitsy pieces and stomp the pieces clear into the ground. But now John was careful not to let his temper get loose if he could help it. Even during his brawl with Brian O'Brian he'd stayed cool when any other man would have been boiling over.

Blanche watched him for a moment, then as John turned around she said quietly, "At first he made me an offer, a cash settlement to divorce Tom and marry him. I told him to—"

John waited, then said, "You rejected his offer?"

"Emphatically." Blanche's lips twisted bitterly. "But it didn't matter. The Colonel's mind was made up."

She stopped and stared down at her hands. "Two weeks later Tom and I rounded up some cattle and started driving them to Santa Fe."

"Santa Fe's over two hundred miles from here," I said. "The two of you couldn't . . ."

She glanced at me and shrugged a little. "We only had a hundred and fifty head. And we had Jimmy to help us. It wasn't hard."

I stared at her in open-mouthed admiration. A man, a woman and an eight-year-old boy. Driving a hundred and fifty longhorns, the wildest, meanest critters God ever created, through miles of rock and sand, blistering heat and blood-crazy Injuns.

John and I looked at each other, agreeing that if a drive like that wasn't hard, it would sure do most folks as a substitute. I wasn't no lily, and I'd eaten my share of trail dust, but just the thought of a drive like that gave me the shakes.

"What happened?" John asked Blanche kinda gentle-like.

She lifted her eyes to look at him, but she was seeing something else.

"The herd was stampeded." Her voice was flat and had no emotion. "Tom was trying to turn the herd. His horse stumbled and fell."

She stopped and I saw a wet shine come into her eyes. But she didn't break down. We just sat there and after a minute or so she said in the same tone of voice, "We buried what we could find of him the next morning."

She stopped again. I wanted to say something, but I couldn't find the right words. Maybe there wasn't any. I knew one thing. I was working up a powerful feeling about a certain ex-Reb colonel. I could see that John was, too.

Blanche finally went on to tell us how she and the boy had rounded up what they could find of the scattered herd. She sold them for what she could get from the nearest rancher. She and Jim had gone back to their ranch, but she couldn't stand living there with all the memories of her husband and the dreams they'd dreamed there, so she'd moved into town and rented this house from Steiner, the storekeeper.

John asked her about relatives, but Blanche shook her head. She had kinfolks back East, and a married sister in Ohio, but she wasn't going to leave. She had a funny look in her eyes when she said it that made me feel like a ghost had just run his fingers down my spine.

"Blanche," said John slowly, "did you see the men who started that stampede?"

She shook her head tiredly.

"Then maybe it was Indians—"

"Indians or white outlaws, why didn't they round up the herd and drive it off? A woman and a little boy couldn't stop them."

John just shook his head, not wanting to believe the truth. But it was plain enough. Blanche made it plainer.

"Ten days after I buried my husband, Belknap rode in to tell me—tell me, mind you—that I was going to marry him as soon as the circuit rider arrived." Blanche took a breath and looked at John steadily. "Do you think the stampede was an accident?"

John hesitated, then let out a long unhappy sigh. "No. But without proof—"

"What good would proof do? Who would arrest him? No federal marshal could arrest Belknap unless invited to do so by the local sheriff. And you know that Tom Maple is owned by Belknap, body and soul!"

"I've heard that," admitted John.

47

There was a miserable silence. I finally stood up and said, "Look, I got a question. What good would it do Belknap to get him a wife that hated his guts like you do?"

"I believe the Colonel's boast," said Blanche, "is that he will have me tamed in a week, pregnant in a month, and devoted in a year."

That was when I had to get out.

VIII

I WAS A REAL PICKER, I was. After nearly thirty years of looking I had to pick Blanche Maginnis to fall in love with. And make no mistake about that, I'd fallen all right, head over hip pockets. Her pug-nosed and freckled face, framed by that thick mahogany-colored hair, was burned so deep in my heart I knew I'd be seeing it in a thousand campfires until I finished my time on this earth. Funny, she was nothing like my dream girl at all. I guess every fellow starts off with a dream girl, you know, a girl he's gonna meet some day who's everything he wants right down to the last detail. For me, the dream girl was a tall blonde with big purple eyes and a quiet easygoing nature. A girl who was all soft and feminine and who was scared to bait her own fishhook.

So look what I picked! A green-eyed redhead who was hardly big enough to spit over a short-legged dog! A girl that wore men's britches and was about as quiet and easygoing as a stick of dynamite with the fuse lit. And if there was anything that scared her I sure hadn't seen it yet. To top it off she was a widow with an eight-year-old kid, though to be honest the boy got to me near as much as she did.

You maybe noticed that john had strong feelings about cussing, so I held off till I was out of the house before I let go. But then I made a workmanlike job of it. I used English, Spanish, border Mex—which is a language all of its own—even some French that I'd picked up from a Creole schoolteacher, a prim-looking little thing and by a wide margin the best all around, no-holds-barred free-style cusser I ever met. The mood I was in I'd have even used Apache, only being nothing but heathen savages their language didn't have no cusswords.

I started off with cussing Saber, Confederate colonels, all Belknaps, all Belknaps from Virginia, Rye W. Belknap in especial particular, all redheads, all little female-type redheads, longhorn cattle, hosses that stumble, and I was working on me, my soft heart, my softer head, when I saw them riding towards me.

They were only a hundred yards or so away by then. Even a mush-headed preacher's nurse like me should have noticed them sooner, but that didn't help now. There were half a dozen of them, and a mean-looking hard-bitten bunch they were, too. Guns and knives hung all over them. I even saw a Sioux pipe-ax sticking out of one black-bearded hardcase's boot. All together they had enough weapons to start a fair-sized war. But it was the man riding out in front all by himself that made the ice slide down my backbone.

He wasn't much for size, even sitting on a big wild-looking uncut stud. Standing in his polished black cavalry boots he might have gone five-and-a-half feet. His uniform was a tailor's work of art, even if the army it represented no longer existed. Having worn a similar uniform some years past I had no trouble recognizing his rank. It was that of a full colonel in the Army of the Confederate States of America. His regalia was complete too, right down to the bright, shiny saber jangling from his belt.

I didn't waste much time looking—about two seconds. Then I spun and legged it fast. Behind me I could hear a voice raised in sharp command.

"Stop! You, there! Stop! Come back here!"

I didn't bother trying to open Blanche's gate. I vaulted it on the run, almost fell on my face, recovered and plunged on into the house.

"Belknap!" I gasped and flung myself on the floor by the front window. I rested the barrel of my gun on the sill and drew the hammer back to full cock. With my left hand I began shucking shells from my cartridge belt to get them handy for reloading.

Blanche, making a kind of snarly sound, jumped for a battered Colt revolving rifle that stood in one corner. John took the rifle from her swiftly.

"No, Blanche!" he said. "Frank, put away that gun!"

I swung my head to gape at him as he pulled the pin and dropped the rifle cylinder into his hand. He put the cylinder into his pocket, leaned the rifle by the door and smiled at me calmly. "Don't be so blood-thirsty, Frank," he said and stepped outside before I could choke out an answer.

"They'll kill him!" whispered Blanche. I swapped

glances with her, agreeing a hundred per cent, then turned back to the window. I'd get Belknap, I swore to myself, no matter what else happened.

Oh, I was all set to go down fighting like a real hero. Which goes to show you just what a jackass a man can make of himself with a woman around.

Colonel Rye W. Belknap stopped his little army in front of Blanche Maginnis' house. He made a curt signal with his left hand and the man directly behind him dismounted and moved to meet my brother.

"Are you Niles?"

John nodded. "I'm the Reverend—"

The man made a chopping motion with his hand. "I'll talk. I'm Lee Overstreet, executive aide to Colonel Rye W. Belknap."

That's what he said, honest to God! John inclined his head then tilted it so he could look at Belknap who was sitting on his dancing stud like he expected Matthew Brady to pop out of the bushes and take his picture any minute.

"Colonel," said John. "Of what army, sir?"

I could have kissed John for that. His soft question sent the red surging up into Belknap's face and for a moment I thought he was going to whip out his saber and go for John. Then he got control and drew himself up coldly.

"Army of the Confederate States of America, retired," said the colonel in a thin metallic voice.

"The Colonel would like to speak with Mrs. Maginnis," Overstreet said quickly. "In private."

"I'll bet he would," John murmured.

Overstreet blinked. His bleached white eyebrows lifted. "What?"

John smiled. "Question is, would Mrs. Maginnis like to speak with the Colonel. I don't really think she would."

Overstreet darted a look at Belknap, then muttered, "You're being unwise, Reverend. We don't want to make trouble."

"That's fine. I'm against it in principle myself."

Until now Overstreet's voice and manner had been soft and polite, but suddenly behind his iron-rimmed spectacles his colorless eyes took on a curious kind of shine. That's when I remembered his name. Lee Overstreet! Ex-marshal, ex-bounty hunter, ex-guerrilla, and plain executioner. He didn't look very dangerous, being a medium-sized man on the slender side, wearing a drab, dusty suit and derby hat, but if he wasn't the deadliest human being alive he was close to it.

Overstreet took off his glasses and blew on them, wiping them with a handkerchief. I shifted my gun sights to him, centering on his belt buckle. With him looking at John the way he was I figured the Colonel could wait.

Belknap shifted in his saddle, leaned forward and spoke flatly. "Reverend Niles, you and your brother have caused me a good deal of trouble already. You have assaulted and injured several of my men—"

"Self-defense, Colonel," retorted John. "A legal as well as moral justification."

Belknap waved that aside. "Not to me, sir. However I prefer to be magnanimous in this case. To take punitive action against a man of the clergy would be most dis-

tressing to me. I hope you won't make such action necessary."

John said nothing.

Belknap frowned and continued, "You understand that I
cannot—and by God, sir, I will not—tolerate interference
in my personal life."

"Naturally," said John. He paused slightly, then his
voice took on a sharp edge. "Mrs. Maginnis was saying
exactly the same thing to me only a moment ago."

Belknap's face went white, then red with terrible fury.
He stood up straight in the stirrups like he was going to
send his black stallion right over the fence at John. "You
righteous fool!" he snarled. He started to draw his saber.
"I'll teach you to—"

"Colonel!"

Overstreet's soft voice seemed to freeze Belknap with
his saber half-drawn. "Not here, Colonel. Not now."

With a shuddering effort painful to see the Colonel got
control of his temper and let his saber slide back into the
scabbard with a steely clink. Slowly he sat back down in
the saddle and shook his head slightly as if dazed. His
burning eyes fastened on John.

"You—you make it hard," he said thickly. "I didn't want
to—"

The sound of a wagon and horses stopped Belknap. I
looked and goggled at what was for sure the fanciest
buggy ever made. Painted a shiny black and gold with
bright red wheels, it had a fringed top with little fluffy
gold balls hanging all the way around. The harness leather
was oiled till it gleamed and the brass hardware was pol-

ished till it'd put a man's eye out. Sitting next to the driver all humped over and looking sicker'n a poisoned pup was a muchly bandaged Scanlan.

When the buggy stopped a man with bushy burnsides hopped out of the back seat and gave Belknap an eager smile.

"Everything all set, sir?"

"No," snapped the Colonel. "Go inside and get her. It's your job, you're the doctor."

"Yes, sir!"

His black bag in hand, the doctor opened the gate and trotted up the walk only to find John blocking his path.

"Excuse me," he said. He took a step, stopped again when John made no move to get out of his way.

"Did Mrs. Maginnis send for you?" John asked.

The doctor was startled and confused by John's blunt inquiry. Glancing helplessly at Overstreet, then Belknap, the doctor said hesitantly, "Well, no, not exactly. That is—"

Overstreet said smoothly, "Colonel Belknap's fiancée has been suffering from a severe nervous condition, isn't that right, Doctor Holly?"

"Hm?" Doctor Holly stared at him blankly, then stammered quickly, "Oh, yes, yes of course. Shock of her husband's death, you know. Upset her mental equilibrium."

"Poor girl suffers from delusions now," said Overstreet sadly. "Even hallucinations. That's why the doctor's decided she must be taken to a place where she can have the proper care and supervision."

"Like Saber Ranch?"

Overstreet smiled at John. "Where else?"

IX

I T WAS LIKE getting hit with a club. It was so rotten, yet so perfect. Holly was the only doctor in Concho. With his support Belknap could shove his plan through and nobody could stop him. And no matter what Blanche said, nobody would believe her. Belknap would even have most folks sympathizing with him. Poor Colonel Belknap, his pretty young fiancée is addled in the head, how sad, how sad.

I wanted to throw up.

Of course once Belknap got Blanche to Saber he'd see to it that she got well in a hurry. Well enough, anyway, so he could force through a marriage as soon as he found a preacher who didn't have John's scruples.

There was only one way to stop a bastard like Belknap, I told myself. I was ready to do it, too, only before I could shoot I had to handle a red-hot little redhead. Blanche had heard Overstreet, same as I had, and when she did she let out a couple of sizzling words no lady ought to know, much less use. Then she started for the door.

I don't know what she figured on doing. Claw Belknap's eyes out probably. It didn't matter, I had to stop her and I did, at the cost of some hide and my chance to blow Belknap's head off.

Outside, John tried to stall things off but the best he could do was to make Doc Holly wait where he was while John came in to get Blanche.

As soon as he was inside John grabbed for Blanche and

pulled her close to whisper rapidly in her ear. I understood that he didn't want the men outside to hear what he was saying but that was no reason why he had to move away when I tried to listen.

"John, do I have to?" pleaded Blanche out loud.

John nodded unhappily. "If you don't go they'll simply take you by force." He added bitterly, "For your own good, of course."

I was back at the window and remembering a previous thought when John shot me a look and emphatic head-shake.

They'd barely gone out when Blanche's scream came, high and terror-stricken, followed by a thumping and clattering sound. For an instant her cry paralyzed me, then I was tearing out the front door with fear clawing my vitals.

Blanche was sprawled at the foot of the porch steps, her slim body all twisted, moaning in agony. John, Doc Holly and Overstreet were all bending over her. I went down the steps in one jump, yanked Overstreet back and spun him aside like a rag doll. I fell to my knees beside Blanche and started to slide my hand under her mop of red hair.

"Don't touch her!" the doctor said sharply. I jerked back my hand and choked out, "It was just a fall, wasn't it Doc? She's not hurt bad, is she?"

Holly grunted, not looking up. "Arms are okay."

"Seems to be her back," said John, his eyes meeting Blanche's briefly. She closed her eyes and groaned.

The doctor finished checking Blanche's arms and started on her legs, carelessly flipping her dress and petticoats halfway up her thighs. I gasped at the sight of Blanche's exposed legs. They were beautiful. Then I stiffened and roared in outrage, "Pull down that dress!"

Holly snapped indignantly, "Oh, don't be a fool! I'm a doctor!"

"Yeah?" I retorted. "Well, the rest of these popeyed gents ain't docs! Pull it down!"

Holly got the point with a glance around him and scowlingly pulled down Blanche's dress, examining her under it by feel. That was bad enough. I watched him with a mean, suspicious eye, trying to keep in mind about him being a doctor, but if his hands had made one funny move I was gonna blow his damm head off, doctor or not. I guess he knew it because he finished her legs in a hurry.

"Legs not broken," he announced, giving me a nervous glance.

Blanche moaned and stirred. "My back—it's my back," she got out between clenched teeth.

Before Holly could do anything further Colonel Belknap became impatient. "Never mind, Doctor. That's enough. You can finish examining her at the ranch."

"But Colonel Belknap, she—"

"Don't argue with me," said Belknap curtly. "Get her into the buggy."

Holly looked at Blanche and hesitated, plainly struggling with his conscience. John was an expert on consciences, so he understood and came to Holly's rescue.

"Doctor Holly," said John in a penetrating voice, "the young lady has suffered a back injury. Don't you know that any unnecessary movement can be dangerous, even fatal?"

The doctor grew red and indignant. "Of course I know it! I'm a—"

"Careful, Doc," murmured Overstreet.

Holly looked at him, swallowed hard and mumbled, "But, I . . . I . . . well, I suppose—"

"You're the one who's going to be held responsible, Doctor Holly," said John.

"I know, I know," groaned the doctor pitifully, "but what else can I do?"

"You can remember your oath and be a man!" John snapped. "I promise you this, if you let that poor girl be taken for a jarring thirty-mile ride in her condition and she dies or her injury is aggravated—to any degree!—you'll spend the next ten years in prison!"

Holly gulped, then very slowly he straightened with a funny gleam brightening his eyes.

"Overstreet! Stop stalling and get her into the buggy!"

Overstreet started to move but Holly put out a hand and stopped him. "No," said Holly. "I'm not going to permit it."

Overstreet turned to pass the buck to Belknap, but the Colonel had heard Holly and shouted, "The devil with what that pill peddler says! We're taking her to the ranch!"

The doctor wheeled on Belknap in surprising belligerence. "You're not! I absolutely forbid it!"

Belknap's eyebrows went up and he leaned forward in the saddle. "You—what?" he demanded.

Holly paled but said flatly, "You're not taking her to Saber until I know she's able to make the trip!"

Again it was Overstreet who cut in to stop Belknap from exploding. Belknap finally snarled at Overstreet, "All right, all right, you stay and handle things. But by God, sir, you better do it right and do it fast." Belknap shot a look of pure hate at Holly and John and added, "Or I'll bring in the whole crew and do it my way!"

After Belknap and company had ridden out, Holly started barking orders for some of the curious towns-people to bring a door and some blankets so Blanche could be carried to his house, a part of which had been converted into a makeshift hospital. It was while they were arranging the blankets on the door and getting ready to shift Blanche onto it that I saw her turn to look at John. She was still letting out groans of pain but her right eye closed in a deliberate wink of triumph!

Sure, sure, I know. I should have caught on that it was a fake fall the minute it happened, but I didn't. Seeing Blanche lying there at the foot of the steps all twisted and moaning—well, it drove any sense I got right out of my head. When I finally did realize it was only a trick John thought up to keep Blanche from being taken to Saber Ranch, I didn't know whether I wanted to kill him or kiss him.

I just stood there gaping at Blanche in tremendous relief until my brother rammed his elbow into my ribs and whispered, "For Pete's sake, Frank, stop grinning! You'll give her away!"

I straightened my face and none too soon. Overstreet was turning to study us with plenty of suspicion already in his eyes. Then with Blanche moved onto the door it was time to carry her to Doc Holly's. He put her to bed in a back room and began shooing us all out of the house like chickens.

At the door Overstreet paused to say, "You'll have her ready to travel as soon as you can, eh Doc?"

"Of course." Holly had been doing some thinking. He tried without success to control a nervous tic in his cheek. He cleared his throat. "I'm only doing my duty as a doctor, Mr. Overstreet. You understand."

Overstreet took off his specs and polished them. "Why, sure. I do. I know you wouldn't try and cross the Colonel." He put on the specs, letting his eyes slide to where I was standing all tense and big-eared. "No smart man would do that, not unless he wanted to die."

My throat felt dry. I knew I was good with a gun. Plenty good. I'd looked through powder smoke more than a few times. I'd seen men go down with my lead in their vitals and I'd been kissed by both lead and steel. Which is why I wanted no part of bracing Overstreet. Only fool kids and idiots went around with that kind of itch. The last thing any smart gunman wanted was a head-to-head shoot-out with one of his own kind. There just wasn't that much difference in the ability of the real gunfighters. Unless you could get a big jump on the other man—and against Overstreet I could just as well wish for the moon—he'd get off a shot or two, with good odds of doing some messy and maybe permanent damage. So while I wasn't going to run from him, I wasn't going to spit in his eye, either, if I could help it.

The doctor, who didn't savvy that Overstreet was

talking mostly to me, had started to quiver pathetically. Overstreet patted his shoulder and gave him a smile that was not much comfort.

"I like you, Doc," Overstreet murmured. "I hope I can get the Colonel to understand. It would be a shame if . . ."

Overstreet patted Holly's shoulder again and sighed, then turned and strolled over to me. He paused and smiled again kind of thoughtfully.

"Niles," he mused. "Frank Niles."

"That's my name."

"I should know a man as good as you are."

"Who said?"

"Lou Scanlan." The corner of Overstreet's mouth twitched. "He was quite impressed."

"That makes my day," I said sourly.

Overstreet's eyes suddenly glinted. "Big Ab! The Texas Deacon! Abner Niles! You're Ab's kid."

"One of them." I shrugged.

"He was great," said Overstreet softly. "Maybe the best there was."

It was an honest compliment and I knew it. For a little bit of time Overstreet and I were not enemies who might kill one another but simply men remembering a man who had walked a little taller than his fellows. At least that's how I remembered Pa. Not just that he was a magician with a gun and a champ fighting man any way you took him, but that he had a kind of bigness about him, call it dignity if you want, that made other men respect him and look to him for leadership. It was the same quality John had. All I got from Pa was his size and maybe some of the magic in my hands.

"If you're half as good as the Deacon, you'll be hard to put down," said Overstreet.

That broke the spell. I gave Overstreet a wolfish grin.

"You know the price of finding out."

Overstreet nodded, smiling crookedly. "When I have to, I'll pay it. But why don't you take your brother and just ride on?"

"How far would we get?"

"My word," said the gunman. "Leave today and Saber won't touch either of you."

I sighed and shook my head. "Can't be done."

"Why? There's nothing to hold you two in Concho!"

I couldn't help it, my eyes naturally flicked to the house. Overstreet didn't miss it. His bleached eyebrows shot up. "Her? You?"

I made no answer. I didn't need to. That one glance was enough giveaway. Overstreet shook his head in amazement. His soft laugh didn't have much laugh in it, but I hated him for it.

"Didn't you hear about her being Colonel Belknap's fiancée?" He chuckled.

"I heard the moon was green cheese, too."

Overstreet frowned. "You know, the Colonel has a pretty bad temper. He wanted to string up both you and your brother after what you did to Scanlan and Cory. I talked him out of it. I don't think I could do it again."

"I doubt it myself."

"Then take some advice. Don't press your luck. It won't stand the strain."

X

D AMMIT, you could have at least let me know what she was going to do!" I grumbled at John. "Hearing her scream and fall nearly gave me a heart attack."

"Don't curse, Frank," said my brother. "I couldn't tell you, you'd have given it away. The way you reacted was the thing that made them believe her fall was real."

We were sitting in the kitchen of Effie Peach's house having a council of war over Effie's coffee and dried peach fritters. On the inside it was just an ordinary kind of cottage, but the outside was something you had to see to believe, if then. After her husband was killed Effie had looked for things to do to keep herself from thinking. She decided to paint her house. Steiner didn't have enough of any one color to do the job, so Effie took what he had and did the job anyway. With the result that her house was white on one side, blue on the other, yellow in front and green in back with a roof that was red as fire. She painted the picket fence and the outhouse with the dabs left from each bucket so they looked like drunken rainbows. It was one helluva sight, let me tell you. Ben Steiner swore he had to shut his eyes every time he visited Effie to keep from getting sick to his stomach and offered to repaint the house any color she wanted, but Effie stubbornly refused. She said she liked it. John told me that he thought she liked all the moaning and groaning people did about it.

Ben Steiner had just brought the news that Colonel

Belknap had sent his housekeeper, Mrs. Spain, to help Doc Holly take care of Blanche.

"And to find out if Blanche is faking," added Ben grimly.

"Well, she is faking, isn't she?" I demanded.

"Of course she is," said John. He smiled suddenly. "It was a beautiful tumble, though. You should have seen it."

I gritted my teeth. "Then she's in a damn bad spot—I know, I know, don't cuss, but dammitall, she is in a bad spot!"

"Not as bad as being a prisoner at Saber Ranch," snapped Effie from the stove where she was dipping candles in a washtub of tallow. Like most women she thought John was perfect.

"But what happens when Belknap finds out she's faking?"

"I don't think he will," John said. "A doctor once told me that a back injury was almost impossible to prove one way or the other. In any case we have some time."

"Time for what?"

"Time to pull that throne from under Belknap. Take his power away from him."

I threw up my hands and groaned. "You're crazy, John! A stark raving idiot! You can't fight Belknap, he's too big!"

"No man's bigger than the law, Frank."

"Law? What law? His?"

"Law is the will of the people, all of them, not one man. No man can own the law."

"Well, he owns the sheriff. Same thing."

John shook his head irritably. "It's not. A sheriff can be replaced."

It was Steiner's turn to shake his head. "With a new election, sure, but we haven't had an election in six years."

"Then it's time you had one," John declared flatly.

"It is," agreed Steiner, "but who's going to organize it? Not me, I'm a coward."

"You are not!" came Effie's rocks-down-a-tin-chute bellow. "And you stop talkin' like that, Benjamin!" When we turned to look at her, her leathery cheeks turned pink, but she said defiantly. "He's as brave as any man in Concho!"

Effie turned back quick to her candle dipping. Steiner scowled at her but he didn't mean it. John lifted his coffee cup to hide a smile, put it down and announced:

"I'm going to do it."

"You?" gasped the rest of us.

"Who's in a better position? I have to visit everyone anyway in the course of my work. Most of them are friendly, I believe all of them trust me, at least enough to listen to what I have to say."

"That's swell," I said. "That's fine. I'll even admit that you can talk birds out of a tree so maybe you can talk people into going against Belknap, too. But there's still two kinda large-type problems. First, who's the man willing to commit suicide?"

Effie and Steiner frowned at me but John said, "You mean, who will be willing to run for the office of sheriff, of course."

"That's what I mean. You know anybody who'll stand up and play target for Saber gunhawks?"

Steiner looked at Effie who looked at John who looked at both of them. After a minute John said slowly, "It will be dangerous—"

I snorted. "Fatal's the word. A good man might last twenty-four hours as a candidate. Get a Hickok or Earp and I'll make it a week."

"No," said John with a headshake. "Concho's not big enough to afford men like that. No, we—"

Effie and Steiner both suddenly said, "Quincannon!"

John threw back his head and laughed. "Scots whae hae! The very mon!"

"Aye, he'll ken what tae do!" said Steiner.

"Nae doot about it," said Effie.

There was more and worse. I don't know what there is about the Scottish accent that makes everybody want to imitate it, but they do. And if you think you've heard it done bad, you should have heard the way Effie's gravelly bass mangled it.

In between and around the miserable dialect I gathered that Cadmus Quincannon had a horse ranch that bordered Saber in the foothills. The old Scot also had four grown sons—as well as a few youngsters—a terrible temper, and a long-standing grudge against Saber. As there were other Scots neighboring him, all clansmen, I had to admit it would make killing Quincannon a rough proposition. For when you down a Scot you have to take on his whole darn clan as well. They're worse than Tennessee back-woodsmen about blood feuds.

"Aye, noo all ye hae tae do is tae talk him intae it, begorra!" Effie rumbled, mixing in some bad Irish to go with her bad Scottish.

"John can do it!" Steiner stated firmly.

John looked over at me and said, "You mentioned two problems, Frank. First, getting the right candidate. What's the other?"

I got up, stretched and muttered gloomily, "Oh, I was just thinking that you didn't really need a candidate."

"Why not?" John demanded.

"Because, you darned fool, when you start this election campaign, Belknap's going to hear about it. When he does he'll finish the campaign for you. And us along with it!"

With that off my chest I stomped out to find me a place where I could cuss and drink something besides coffee.

X I

THERE WAS A CHOICE of five saloons and three cantinas in Concho. I headed for the nearest and biggest, the Oriental Palace, which looked about as oriental as a hot dog and for sure wasn't no palace, but I was in no mood to be picky. I wasn't even in a mood to have good sense. I clink-clumped right past a line of hosses all wearing the Saber brand without seeing a thing. If that wasn't enough I barged right into the saloon and went right up to the bar like a man who's downright tired of living.

Usually I was a fairly careful sort of fellow, and I had the fact that I was twenty-nine and breathing to prove it.

I'd tried to make it a habit when entering dim saloons from bright sunlight to step quick to one side and keep my back to the wall till I could see who and what was waiting for me inside. That may sound like a silly kind of habit, but let me tell you, brother, there were times when it meant all the difference between a long life and a fast funeral.

This was one of those times.

That I found out when my eyes finally started focusing. The saloon wasn't any surprise. I'd seen a hundred just like it all over the Territory. Rammed earth floor covered with sawdust, zinc-topped planked bar with a long, cracked and wavy mirror on the wall behind it. Maybe a dozen tables and a bunch of chairs that had been busted and wired together so many times a man had to be dead tired or dead drunk to sit down on one. But in the mirror I saw that I had company I could have done without. Six Saber hardcases who were looking at me like I was already dead and just hadn't been covered up yet.

If they weren't enough Lee Overstreet himself was standing by a corner table talking to Brian O'Brian, whose face was something to scare little kids with. Both his eyes were so puffed and swollen it was a wonder he could see at all. The skin of his big nose had been scraped off, and somebody had been plenty free with iodine and sticking plaster. I wouldn't even try to describe the colors of his face except to say that he looked like an ugly Piute who'd put on his war paint at night while blind drunk and standing on his head.

For a minute everybody was frozen still, then Overstreet

tossed a few pieces of gold on the table in front of Brian and said, "All right, Brian, it's your decision. But don't hang around. Make long tracks and make them fast."

Overstreet turned and walked to the others, who were starting to get up and move in my direction. The white-faced bartender put up a palm pleadingly, backing off down the counter.

"Now, fellows, please—not here, fellows. Go outside—please, fellows, don't shoot in here. My mirror . . . glasses . . . my furniture . . ."

Overstreet frowned at the Saber riders. "Boys, you know what the Colonel said."

A squat, red-bearded man grated, "The Colonel's not my compadre, Cory is."

A tall, scar-faced gunhawk said, "Lou Scanlan's mine."

"You know the score, Lee," said one with the pouchy cheeks of a mean squirrel. "Let him get away with it and pretty soon every drunk with a grudge is taking shots at Saber men. Bad enough to let the preacher off."

"We'll have to make this one example enough for two," grinned Redbeard.

Overstreet glanced my way and shrugged. "All right. He's yours, but no guns, no knives. That way it can be passed over as just a fight."

Overstreet strode from the saloon. I backed off down the bar a ways but the Saber men moved with me, keeping that half-circle advantage. I kept my hand well away from my gun. They'd probably obey Overstreet if I didn't force them to use weapons. If I did, no matter how many I could put down I'd end up a corpse. The other way there was a chance of coming through alive. Not much chance but better than none at all.

All six of them moved at once. I hooked my elbows over the bar and brought my legs up doubled, kicked out hard. I caught Redbeard and the man next to him just as they sprang forward, my boots striking below their belt buckles with solid impact. Their mouths flew open and they went flying back to go down in a crashing welter of tables and chairs. Behind me I heard the bartender let out a cry of dismay. Then I was nearly swarmed under.

The only thing that saved me was them all trying to slug me at once. They kept getting in each other's way, while I belted everything in reach. Squirrel-cheeks came slamming up against me, his fist pounding my left ear and making things go dizzy while he clawed for my throat with his free hand. I tromped on his foot with my bootheel and then brought up my knee hard. I caught him right in the family jewels and I must have damm near gelded him the way he screeched. He folded under the feet of the others and was kicked aside callously. I nailed Scarface with a beautiful hook on the point of his chin and that was when someone threw a fist that like to tore my nose right off my face.

Have you ever taken a hard punch right on the nose? It doesn't knock you out, but for shock value it can't be beat. Fire flashes into your brain, you go blind and the tears flow and you can't stop there, and you hurt like hell all over.

I'd felt the cartilage break. I knew my nose was busted again. I threw my arms up, trying to cover up, move away, stall at least till I could see again. They really pounded me then. One trained fist-fighter could have slaughtered me. As it was I caught a lot of the punishment on my forearms and elbows and managed to stay on my feet somehow. I knew that if they ever got me down it would be all over but the flowers and sad music. Screwiest thing about it was that I kept worrying about how bad my nose was broke, would it make me look so ugly Blanche couldn't stand it, or could the doc straighten it a little? Which is a hell of a way to be thinking when a half-dozen plug-uglies are doing their best to unscrew your head.

Someone hit me on the neck with what felt like a sledge hammer and when I sagged I knew it was the beginning of the end. My knees kept buckling and I was going down, then over the howls of triumph I heard a roar that was familiar.

"Argggg, 'tis sick I am of watching ye bunch of white-livered dogs all chewin' on one dacent fightin' man!"

My eyes stopped watering enough for me to see Brian O'Brian wading into the knot of Saber men as they started using their boots on me. Swinging his great fists like anvils the big Irishman smashed into the bewildered hard-cases and toppled them like tenpins.

Reaching me he put down an enormous hand and yanked me to my feet with a grimace I took to be a grin.

"Up and at 'em, laddiebuck! 'Tis no time to be sittin' around on yer duff!"

Somewhere in the back of my mind I had the thought that Brian was fighting on the wrong side, but there was no time to do any wondering about that. A high-pocketed

Saber hand busted a chair over Brian's skull when he turned from helping me. It would have put the average man in bed for a month but all Brian did was shudder and shake it off with a bellow of rage. Grabbing the chair-wielder by the arm he spun and heaved and sent the man sailing clear over the bar to smash the mirror into a jillion pieces and cause the little barkeep to shriek in misery.

I fought my way out from the bar only to be tripped and go down again. I was barely up when I saw Redbeard charging me like a mad buffalo, his hand sprouting ten inches of bowie knife. I recalled one of Pa's wrestling tricks and grabbed Redbeard's outstretched wrists, let myself fall backwards, doubling my legs. Planting my feet in his belly I yanked him hard, then straightened my legs as he shot over me. He kinda sailed through the air till he came to the wall. I thought for a minute he was going out the window but he was too high for that. He plowed through the thin plank wall instead. Part-way through he stopped and just sort of hung there, half in and half out of the saloon but clear out of the fight.

Brian bellowed in delight, "That's me boy!" He grabbed the nearest Saber man and lifting him high, Brian hurled him like a sack of potatoes towards the front. The man hit the swinging doors with a crash, went on, taking the doors with him.

From there on it was all ours. I racked one up in the corner, turned and saw Scarface backing away from Brian and whipping out his pistol. I snatched up a broken chair leg and spun it through the air in time to hit his arm and send the shot wild. Then Brian was on him like a panther, grabbed and heaved, and after the crash Scarface slid down the wall in an unconscious heap.

Brian stood there panting, looking for more enemies. All that was left was Squirrel-cheeks, who was rolling around on the floor holding himself and making pitiful cries. Brian stalked over to him.

"Ah, now ye poor tyke, ye're in pain," he rumbled. "Here, let me help."

Scooping up the groaning hardcase Brian held him at arm's length, measured him and belted him on the chin, knocking him colder than last week's cinders.

"Ye see?" said Brian. "Now ye feel better." With that Brian tossed the man aside carelessly. Squirrel-cheeks landed on a table that collapsed in a heap of splintered wood.

Brian came over to where I was holding on to the bar. He pounded on the zinc. "Ollie!" he roared. "Thirsty men stand here waitin' for succor, ye little spalpeen! Show yer-self!"

XII

OLLIE DANE'S white popeyed face appeared over the far end of the bar.

"Is it over?" he squeaked.

"All over! Start pourin'."

Ollie pointed at me. "But he's still alive!"

"And thirsty! Set out a bottle and glasses."

Ollie ignored Brian, his horror-stricken eyes roving over his shattered property.

"Demolished! Everything! Completely demolished!" He groaned. "It'll take weeks to wire things back together!"

Brian said soothingly, "Well, at least we spanked the demolishers for ye this time, Ollie."

Ollie jerked around to glare at him. "Yes! By God, you did that! I won't forget it either! Here! You two need a drink of my special!"

He bent and brought up a bottle, poured two tumblers brimming full.

"Drink up, my friends!"

I stopped feeling my throbbing nose, picked up the drink and dumped it down my throat gratefully. Then I held on tight to the bar as my innards turned into paralyzing white-hot flame. My eyes bulged out, tears started running down my cheeks again while thirteen little devils started prying off the top of my head. I shuddered and gasped for breath, blindly hoping for death to come quick. Through the roaring in my ears I vaguely heard a voice.

"On the house to my friends."

My eyes slowly stopped watering and a face swam into focus. It was smiling at me.

"If you're a friend," I managed to whisper through my seared throat, "how come you poisoned me?"

The face made a face and chuckled.

"Does have kind of a nip to it, doesn't it?"

"Nip, hell!" I grunted hoarsely. "That stuff bites worse than a full-grown grizzly bear. What is that, distilled dynamite, anyway?"

The face grew a neck and shoulders and finally became

Ollie Dane again. He smiled and said, "My own special recipe. It's wonderful for hangovers, shaky knees and jumpy tummies. Have some more."

He poured again for both of us but I backed off and shuddered. I wasn't about to swallow any more of that liquefied hell voluntarily. I looked at Brian and saw that he was gripping the bar with both hands, staring at his drink glassily.

"'Tis the Holy Grail! I've found it at last!" Brian's puffy eye slits rose to Ollie. "Why, ye're a genius, lad! A genius!"

Ollie looked pleased but waved it aside modestly. After we swapped names around I discovered the reason for Ollie's hatred for Saber. Seemed that he'd had a big lazy mongrel dog, not much of an animal. Ollie admitted the dog's only virtues were his friendliness and his enormous capacity for lager beer.

"Not that he was a drunk, mind you," Ollie explained. "Amigo always held his beer like a gentleman. Everybody loved Amigo."

Everybody except Colonel Belknap. When Amigo had bounded out to greet Belknap one day, the stud had shied and nearly unseated the Colonel. As soon as he got the stallion under control Belknap had drawn his saber and deliberately killed the dog with one powerful slash of the blade. The Colonel and his crew had ridden on, laughing about it, but they'd left behind them a kind of hate I hope nobody ever feels for me.

"I ain't the bravest soul in the world," Ollie said quietly, "but if I ever see Belknap without that crew around him

I'll make him pay for murdering Amigo."

He dropped his hand behind the bar to pat something and when I took a look I saw it was a sawed-off double barreled ten-gauge Greener. Ollie probably wasn't much of a gunman, but me, I'd back a baby with a shotgun against Wes Hardin himself. You don't need to be good with a sawed-off shotgun, you just point, pull, then go start digging graves for the people you've killed.

"Say, what the hell's happened in here, anyway?" came a high-pitched whine.

Ollie showed his dislike openly. "Go someplace else, Fisher. I'm closed."

A man with a narrow pinched face and sharp black ferret eyes swaggered up to the bar. He rang down a double eagle.

"'S matter," he sneered, "ain't my money as good as theirs? Gimme a couple of bottles of your best and a double shot of the same."

Ollie sighed but went to serve him.

"Who's our friend with the bum ears?" I asked Brian.

The giant shrugged. "Mark Fisher. Used to work for Belknap as bookkeeper. Retired a couple of years ago."

"Retired? At his age?" I gave Fisher another look, noticing his expensive clothes, the flashy diamond on his pinky. "What's his secret?"

Brian looked startled; then glancing around, he muttered, "'Tis no joke, laddiebuck. Fisher has one and it pays him fine wages, too."

It was my turn to look startled. "From Belknap?"

"Ivery month he's receivin' hundreds in gold from the

Colonel. I've seen it with me own eyes."

"He must know where the body's buried," I said, watching the dudish Fisher saunter out.

Brian shook his head slightly. " 'Tis anyone's guess—"

He stopped and reached for his glass.

"Drink up fast, laddiebuck. The sheriff's come in and I don't think he's goin' to be so happy with us."

Without thinking I grabbed the glass before me and tossed it down. I started to turn, grabbed Brian and hung on desperately while the Battle of Shiloh was fought all over again in my belly and my throat fused into a solid pillar of fire. Now you'd think that going through a thing like that twice—and after a hard fight, too—would be enough misery for one man, but through the roaring fog I heard a man's voice lifting angrily.

"Put your hands up! You're under arrest!"

XIII

I WAS NOT DRUNK!" I howled bitterly.

"Shhh, Frank, it's all right, now drink your coffee," said John, but his sad eyes still reproached me.

"But I wasn't! Tell him, Brian!"

Sitting beside me on the narrow jail cot Brian guzzled steaming coffee from a tin cup, his puffy eye slits on John. The Irish giant looked like he'd been run through a rock crusher. He was a dreadful mess. Of course John didn't look any too good himself. I didn't know what I looked like but I could guess. My nose felt about nine times its normal size and made me talk thick and mushy.

John said, "He told me, Frank. I said it's all right."

"You didn't say you believed me," I complained. "And it's true. I hadn't had a drink when those cutthroats jumped me. If it hadn't been for Brian—" I stopped, looked at Brian suspiciously. "Say, how come you fought on my side? You're a Saber hand!"

Brian took his face from his coffee cup long enough to mumble, "Not any more. I quit. I don't like pushin' women around."

John smiled at him warmly. "I knew you were too good a man to do that."

Brian looked at him, touched his jaw, winced, remembering. "Sure, and ye're a fair man yerself, Rivirend. If you preach as hard as you punch, 'tis hard to see how the divil stays in business."

"He cheats," I said.

Brian's laughter was awesome. He rared back and let it come out full and booming, bellowing so loud and long my head hurt. I got up from the cot and glared at him.

"Aw, the hell with you," I muttered.

He grabbed my arm and pulled me back, choking out, "Wait, laddiebuck, wait! What did I do?"

I sneered at him morosely. "With all the misery we've got, the least you could do is feel miserable, but no, you've got to sit around guffawing like a buffalo getting his feet tickled."

A suspicious rumbling came out of Brian, and I muttered, "Go ahead, you big gorilla, start laughing again and I'm moving to a different cell."

The rumbling quieted down finally. John put his own

face under strict control and said, "I've just talked to Doctor Holly—"

"How is she?" I asked quickly. "I mean, I know she's all right, but—"

"I talked to him about the men you were fighting," said John sternly.

"Oh."

"Three of them were only bruised. They're all right—"

Brian scowled. "That many?"

Which got him included in John's look of disapproval. John took a breath and said, "The others are seriously injured. One has several broken ribs and his arm broken in two places, another has a broken jaw, a broken collarbone and a fractured skull among other injuries."

That would be Redbeard, I thought to myself with satisfaction.

"And there's one man who—" John stopped suddenly, a red tinge sliding up into his face. "Who . . . whose uh . . . organs were so badly crushed he'll be in bed for weeks, and he may never be able to uh . . . father any children—"

"They wouldn't want him for a father anyway," I muttered.

"It's nothing to joke about," said John, "causing other men to suffer such injuries. Granted they're not good men—"

"Grant something else too, John," I snapped.

"What's that?"

"They were out to make an example of me. A dead example."

John looked shocked as I told him how the Saber men

had made plain their intentions of beating me to death. Then his jaw set hard and his lips thinned to a straight white line.

"In that case the sheriff was wrong to arrest you," John said quietly, "and he's certainly not going to keep you in jail!"

John rattled the cell door. We heard steps, then Tom Maple's belly came into the room. It always came in first, the sheriff's belly. Not that it was a big one, it wasn't. And it wasn't soft and fat like most but hard and round. The rest of Maple being kinda skinny, it looked exactly like he'd just swallowed a cannonball. It bounced when he walked and jiggled when he talked. Of course there was more to Maple than his belly, but it was what people looked at. They couldn't help it.

"You done talkin' to these sinners, Reverend John?" the sheriff chuckled. He unlocked the cell door.

"More sinned against than sinning," corrected John grimly. "Did you know that they were defending themselves? That they were attacked by those six Saber men?"

Maple blinked at John and scratched his bulbous nose. "Well, I . . . didn't hear it 'zactly that way, Rev—"

"It's true."

"Oh, well I ain't doubtin' your word, but uh, well, what is it you're gettin' at?"

John drew himself up and took a breath. "Being true, then it means they are innocent. Don't you understand?"

The sheriff cocked his head, scratched his nose again, patted his belly as if making sure it was still there and said, "Why, sure, but I still don't see what you're gettin' at."

I could see the flush mounting the back of John's neck but he kept his voice under control.

"It is a principle of law. The law you represent, Sheriff. Innocent men cannot be kept in jail."

"Oh."

"So I'm taking my brother and Mr. O'Brian with me," stated John flatly. "Please get their personal belongings."

Maple nodded, then caught himself with a jerk. "Hey! You mean—oh, no you don't! I 'rested them two and they're gonna stay 'rested!"

"But they've committed no crime!"

"What's that got to do with it?"

John shook his head, a little dazed. Then like he was explaining to a kid he said, "When an officer of the law deliberately acts contrary to the law, he commits two felonies."

"Two what?"

"Crimes. And they will cost you seven years in the Territorial prison."

Maple jumped like he'd been stung. "Prison? Me? That's crazy! I'm the sheriff!"

"Judge Poole has a special dislike for law officers who betray their oath of office. He's a friend of mine, too."

Maple stared at John like he'd suddenly sprouted horns and a long pointy tail. The sheriff licked dry lips, mumbled, "Colonel Belknap would be sore as hell if I turned them loose."

"Don't curse, please. He wouldn't lift a finger to keep you out of prison."

"Well, now I dunno—"

"You think Colonel Belknap would publicly support a criminal? You think he'd admit that the reason a sheriff betrayed his oath and broke the law was to please him?"

"Hell, no!" muttered Maple irritably. "Not him."

All in all it took John about twenty minutes to do the job. It wasn't the best talking job I've seen him do, but it got me and Brian out of jail and started some deep cracks in the sheriff's relationship with Belknap. I was plenty satisfied and Brian was regarding John in childish awe mixed with a heaping portion of plain hero worship.

"Are ye sure now that he's not Irish?" whispered the giant as we left the jail.

"We had the same father and mother," I said. "I'm sure."

Brian shook his head. "A golden tongue like that and he's not even kissed the Blarney stone." He heaved a deep rumbling sigh. "'Tis a beautiful Irishman he'd made."

I just growled at him. I was beginning to feel some of my aches and pains, and they warned me that it wouldn't be long before I'd be too sore to move. I was giving happy thought to some hot grub and a nice soft bed when John took all the joy out of life.

"You better both come with me," he said. "In case the sheriff starts thinking and decides he made a mistake."

There was some argument, mostly by me, mostly about not wanting to leave Blanche there alone in that doctor's house. John wouldn't listen. He said that Mrs. Spain wouldn't let anyone but Jim see Blanche, and as far as us staying around to make sure Belknap didn't bother her, John surveyed us wryly.

"If it came down to a fight," he drawled, "in our condition all three of us put together couldn't lick a badtempered jack rabbit."

While Brian was guffawing like an idiot donkey I took a look at us and had to agree that John was right. We were wrecks.

Which is why the three of us were soon riding out of town, heading for the mountains and a clan of transplanted Highland Scots by the name of Quincannon.

X I V

WE RODE HARD, hanging on grimly, wanting to get as far from Concho as we could before stopping. We made twelve miles before the three of us collapsed at Diamondback Creek. For three hours not one of us stirred; then John—bless his loving heart—managed to move enough to get a tiny smokeless fire going under our battered coffeepot. He was slicing bacon into the frying pan when the combined smells forced me and Brian to stir and sit up.

Brian drew in about a bushel of air and moaned, "Sure and we're in heaven, laddiebuck."

"Try to move," I said.

He did and promptly let out a squawk of agony. I managed a grin of sorts and said, "You see? You haven't made it yet, buster."

The two of us crawled to the creek and doused our heads in the snow-cold water and crawled back to the fire, shivering like a couple of dogs passing peach seeds. John silently poured tin cups full of steaming black coffee. He handed them to us with no word of comment, bless his kind heart, and went back to slicing bacon.

From : his saddlebag John took a sack of potatoes and onions and began slicing them into the pan into the bacon grease. By the time Brian and I had finished the pot of coffee John had our shares divided on a tin plate while he ate his out of the frying pan. John finished first and took the pot to the creek, washed it out and refilled it with water. Putting it on the coals he dumped in a handful of Arbuckle's, took a look at us and added another handful.

Brian and I finished the food and a second pot of coffee, fell back, rolling smokes and feeling like maybe there was some reason to live after all. John rose and stretched, wincing at the pull of sore muscles, then hunkered to feed more twigs to the little fire.

"Brian," he said slowly, "how do you feel about Colonel Belknap?"

I quick put a hand on Brian's arm. "No cussing, though."

Brian swallowed what he'd started to say and growled, "The man's a divil and bad cess to him. Why d'ye ask, Rivirind?"

"I need your help." John went on to explain his plan for organizing the election of a new sheriff, then said, "There's one thing more which is needed to bring about Colonel Belknap's downfall."

"What's that?"

"Evidence. Proof of some crime he's committed." John waved his hand. "Oh, I know there are many things

84

people are certain he's responsible for, but proving them in court would be practically impossible. What we need is evidence, witnesses who will testify—"

"Testify against Belknap?" Brian wagged his head gloomily. "Ye're askin' too much, Rivirind. They'd know the Colonel would be closin' their mouths with a bullet long before they ivir reached the court."

"There must be somebody with the courage to tell the truth!" John protested.

Brian shrugged his massive shoulders. "I'd be willin' to try for ye, Rivirind, but I know of no ividence ye could use in a court."

John kept at him, digging and probing this way and that. Brian did the best he could to think of something helpful, but it was a washout until Brian happened to mention Mark Fisher, Concho's mystery man, who'd apparently figured some way to live off Belknap without working.

John dropped the rest and pressed for everything Brian could tell him about Fisher, and knowing John I could see that he was on the trail of something hot. There wasn't much that Brian knew for sure. Fisher had worked for Belknap as a bookkeeper and did whatever paper work and letter writing had to be done. After three years he suddenly quit. He'd bought himself a beautiful little ranch near town where he played at breeding fast, blooded hosses. Brian had seen Overstreet meet Fisher in town several times and each time Overstreet handed over what looked like several hundred dollars in gold. Once Fisher had ridden out to Saber headquarters and talked to Belknap personally. It hadn't been a friendly talk. Fisher had been cocky and demanding, the Colonel mad. According to Brian the Colonel had finally gone into the house and came out with a small buckskin sack. Belknap had flung the sack at Fisher so viciously it had burst open and several double eagles had spilled into the dirt. When Fisher had picked up the gold and was riding away, the Colonel had snatched up a rifle and leveled on him. Overstreet had stopped Belknap from murdering Fisher, taking the rifle away from the Colonel.

"When did that happen?" John asked.

"Month after he quit."

"Now, try and remember, Brian. Did anything unusual happen just before Fisher left Belknap?"

Brian dug his boot toe into the dirt, his lopsided face twisted in the effort of remembering. He was starting to shake his head when he stopped and blurted, "The Army herds!"

John drilled questions at him and Brian explained that the summer before Fisher quit, Belknap had sold a big herd of cattle to the Army. It was delivered to a detachment of soldiers at Sulphur Springs, to be driven by them to Fort Sumner. But two nights later Indians had stampeded the herd right over the trooper's camp and shot down the few soldiers that escaped the stampede. The Army, being desperate for beef, had contracted with Belknap for a second herd, which had been delivered by a Saber crew. What made Brian suspicious of it was that Overstreet and a dozen picked men had handled both drives, but none of the men were good cowhands. They were all good gunfighters.

" 'Tis me own private opinion," rumbled Brian, "that the Army bought the same herd twice."

John stared at Brian with a thin smile starting to curl the corner of his mouth, his one good eye glinting.

"That's it, Brian. Exactly what we need!"

I couldn't see that. "How do you figure, John? With the soldiers dead, you couldn't prove it."

"You're forgetting our friend, Mister Fisher," replied my brother. "He has the proof! That has to be what he's holding over Belknap's head!"

"Sure," I agreed, "but that doesn't help us none. Fisher ain't about to hand that proof over to us."

John stood up straight, his face darkening. "He's got to, Frank!"

Brian and me exchanged glances. I flipped my cigarette into the fire and pulled my aching body upright. "Let's go have a little talk with Fisher. He didn't look unbreakable."

Brian's chuckle was not a happy sound. "I know a few tricks to be persuadin' a man's tongue to wag. 'Tis but—"

"Stop that kind of talk right now!" John exploded angrily. "You punch-happy heathen! Go back to jail. You should be locked up in cages!"

"Now, just a dammed minute, John," I snarled back at him. "You're forgetting about Blanche. If you think I'm going to let her get forced into marrying Belknap on account of you've got religion, you better think again! If it'll save Blanche I'll cut Fisher's dammed head off!"

"You'll do no such thing and stop cursing!"

"I'll cuss all I dammed well please!"

"You will not!"

"I will too, dammit! I'm a grown man—"

"Then talk and act like one. Not like some bloody savage!"

"You keep talking that way and I'll whup your ass, John Niles!"

"You keep talking that way and you'll have to!"

I glared at him and he glared back at me, squaring off with his fists doubled even though he knew I could lick him. I knew it too, but I also knew it'd be one hell of a job and every muscle in my body groaned at the thought of it. Which was why I swallowed what I started to say and said, "All right, so I'll stop cussing if you'll kindly tell me how we can make Fisher turn loose of whatever he's got against Belknap."

John relaxed with a sigh of relief but shook his head. "I don't know, Frank. But if we'll use our brains instead of brutality, we'll find an answer."

"What makes you so sure?" I demanded.

"I'm going to pray about it," said John simply. "God's never failed me yet. If I do all I can first, He'll take care of the rest of it."

That was my brother's religion in a nutshell. And while like I've said before I'm not terrible religious, I'll admit I got down on my knee bones right alongside John there on that creek bank. I'd seen too many of John's prayers get answered to knock the idea. I don't know exactly how it worked, but I know there's a lot more power in praying than most people ever get wise to. And the way I saw it, if my praying would help even a little bit I wasn't too proud to take a whack at it.

Brian didn't say nothing, but I reckon he must have felt about the same, because he got down on his knees too. We probably made a strange-looking sight, all three of us being battered and tore up like we were. But John, he always said that God never paid no attention to what folks looked like on the outside. It was inside that counted. Of course I knew I wasn't the shiniest fellow that way, either, but I tell you one thing, there wasn't nobody that ever prayed harder or more honest than I was praying that afternoon.

X V

WHEN WE LEFT Diamondback Creek both me and Brian were watching John for some sign that he might be getting a message from his Boss. All I could see was that John was doing his part and trying as hard as he could to figure out an answer to our problem about Fisher.

John caught us staring at him and grinned wryly. He told us to have some patience. In John's book that was the number one virtue. Patience.

We were headed towards Cadmus Quincannon's ranch in the foothills making stops along the way so that John could take care of his duties. When he finished his preacher business he talked hard about having a new election. There wasn't no doubt about it, John stirred up their thinking machines. People liked the idea of having some real law and order in Concho basin. They all made it plain, though, that they thought John was biting off more than he or anybody else could chew. We stopped at Piggy Dean's overnight, and the suet-faced hog rancher added sourly, "Only question is, Reverend John, be how far you'll git afore the Kurnel's men blow ninety-one holes in yore carcass."

"A man who's afraid to fight for his rights," said John, "doesn't deserve any rights."

Piggy grunted. "Yore carcass. I won't bleed none if it gits shot full of holes."

The stink of the hogs was so heavy you could nearly taste it even in the house, and Piggy's hospitality consisted of three straw pallets on the floor of the kitchen— the rest of the house was bulging with big and little Deans—but the three of us could have slept on bare rocks that night. We didn't stir for nine hours. It would have been longer but at daybreak Piggy was outside slopping hogs and the noise was enough to bust the ears off a brass monkey. Squealing and grunting, Piggy yelling and slop buckets banging, it brought me to my feet reaching for a gun.

I stood there swaying and peering around blearily for somebody to shoot. My skull was pounding like all my relatives were inside digging for gold. I didn't know any one man could hurt so much in so many places. John pushed himself to a sitting position, groaning, trying to get his one good eye open enough to see.

Brian was up but he wasn't even trying to open his eyes yet. He stood with his legs spread, holding himself up by hanging on to the stove. The muzzle of his huge Walker Colt wavered its aim all over the kitchen.

"Injuns?" he mumbled.

I started to shake my head, decided not to chance it, and mumbled back at him, "Pigs."

"Oh."

"And Piggy."

"Oh."

"Make coffee."

"Where's stove?"

"You're holding on to it."

"Oh."

Somehow Brian got the Walker stuck back in his waistband without shooting himself and began fumbling around the stove for the coffeepot. John had his eye open now and made it to his feet. He regarded us without fondness.

"You two look awful," he croaked.

"What's that racket?"

"Pigs. Piggy," I muttered.

John staggered to the sink, stuck his head under the pump and worked the handle. It was rusty and shrieked and clanked at every stroke. Brian stiffened and shuddered violently. I tried to stuff a dish towel in my ears and said bad things.

John straightened with water and hair streaming down over his face. He dried himself and finger-combed the hair out of his eyes, the good one squinting at me and Brian.

"Awful," he repeated. "No self-respecting, sincere minister should let himself be seen with such low roughnecks."

Brian was still at the stove, holding the coffeepot in one hand. He stood there staring at it like he was hypnotized. John went over, took the pot from Brian's hand and led him to a chair. Then John stirred up the banked fire, stuffed in wood and started making coffee.

I sagged into a chair still trying to think of a good answer to John's insult. My brain wouldn't tick a tick. It was too busy listening to all the complaints from the rest of my body. Missus Dean and her oldest daughter came into the kitchen to take over from John. They soon had food smells fighting the hog stink and poured muddy, scalding coffee into us by the gallon.

Both females made sympathetic noises at us and did their best to get us awake and feeling better. The daughter kept giggling when she looked at us, but I couldn't blame her for that. If I'd been someone else, and I wished I was right then, I'd have probably haw-hawed.

Believe it or not, John went out to help Piggy with the hogs and to talk with him some more before we left. John was working hard at his election campaign, though if it'd been me I'd have given Piggy back to his pigs.

It wasn't the election I was stewing about. I wanted to get my hands on Fisher and find out if he really did have the deadwood on Belknap. I wasn't going to wait much longer, neither.

As it happened I didn't have to. Riding away from Piggy Dean's, Brian pulled his huge bony sorrel over close to me and poked me in the ribs. I looked and he nodded at John. I saw what he meant. John had a kind of contented smile on his mug. He had the answer, sure as gophers dig holes!

I rammed the hooks into Slug and sent the gray lunging around in front of John and pulled him up hard.

"You got it, ain't you?"

John nodded and said quietly, "It's so obvious we should have seen it immediately."

"So make it obvious to me," I demanded in a tone that was abrasive with impatience. John replied with a question.

"If we're right about Fisher, why hasn't Belknap had him killed?"

Not having any brilliant answers I scowled and grunted, "You're the brains, tell me."

"He's afraid to. Fisher's a crook, but he's not a fool. He knew that Belknap would kill him in a minute if he thought it would solve his problem. So Fisher made sure it wouldn't."

"How?"

John shrugged. "Probably made arrangements with someone to hold the evidence and send it to the authorities if anything happens to him. And of course he made sure Belknap knew this."

I hardly heard John's last few words. Bells were going off in my skull, lights flashing. I wanted to laugh and yell in savage triumph. I drew my Spencer carbine from its boot and checked the loads.

"What do you think you're going to do with that?" asked John sharply.

I stared at him in surprise and said, "What the h— what do you think? You said Fisher made arrangements in case anything happened to him. Well, something's going to! Something about a .56 caliber!"

John threw up his hands despairingly and groaned, "Is that all you ever think of, killing and bloodshed?"

I glared at my brother furiously. "Don't start that again! Dammit all, you came up with the idea yourself—"

"Not to commit murder, and stop cursing!"

"But you said it yourself—" I stopped and took a long deep breath. "Okay, okay, so you make it clear, will you? If we don't kill him—"

"All we have to do is make it look like he's been killed!" John flung at me.

"Of course! Why, sure!" I sneered. "I suppose you've got it all figured out how we can do that little thing."

"I have and I'll tell you if you'll shut up and listen for a minute."

I shut up and I listened. It took more than a minute but when John finished laying out his plan I had to admit it would probably work. One thing I liked about it especially was that it'd give us a chance to make sure we were right. So far we'd been doing some pretty tall and fancy guessing about Fisher. We'd taken a button and sewn a big vest on it. I'd feel a whole lot better once I knew how those guesses stacked up as truth.

If the guesses were wrong we were going to be like a man facing a mad grizzly with a gun big enough to blow him to smithereens—but no shells.

As we rode for Fisher's place John spoke to Brian, suggesting that he had no reason to risk his neck any further. He'd been a big help but it wasn't really his fight and

Overstreet had definitely warned Brian to move on. Brian's face distorted into an injured expression and he quoted from something John had said to a rancher named Hendricks the day before.

"Sure and 'tis not true thin, what ye said about freedom bein' the business of iviry man?"

John opened his mouth, found he had no answer and shut it again. Brian continued:

"Ye said that freedom and justice have to work for all men—or they don't work at all. I believed ye, Rivirind."

"Thank you, Brian," muttered John.

He said no more to Brian about leaving.

X V I

IF JOHN was right about a man being what he feels in his heart I turned hoss thief the minute I laid eyes on the stock running around in Fisher's pasture. Maybe a hundred and fifty or so of the leggiest, sleekest, runningest-looking animals I'd ever clapped my peepers on. No mustangs those hosses! Not with those deep chests and long legs. They were blooded racers with the Barb's influence showing in their heads especially, with their little muzzles "fit to drink from a pint pot" like them Ayrabs say.

Slug pretended to shy from tumbleweeds and nearly threw me into a clump of cholla with his sideways lunge. I yanked him back into the trail, and cussed him under my breath. Jealous devil! Slug never had liked me looking at other hosses. Having me looking at a hundred and fifty of them must have galled him more than he could stand.

We eased down into a clump of alders behind Fisher's house and dismounted to go the rest of the way on foot. Brian and me went ahead, John staying back till we called him. Fisher knew John, but he'd only seen me once and that was with Brian. It wasn't likely Fisher knew Brian had quit so with any luck he'd take us both to be working for Belknap.

It being way past ten o'clock there was only one of Fisher's crew around, a hobbling old ex-buster who did the cooking and chores. One look at us and he stopped moving, his eyes sticking out and big as cartwheels.

"Wh-wh-whut yu fellers want?"

"Hurt you to walk, Pop?" I asked.

The bulging eyes blinked at me. "Only muh pride ah reckon. Why?"

"Want you to take a little hike. That way, towards town." I pointed at the road leading to Concho. From where we were it led straight up a four- or five-mile grade, visible all the way to the top. "You walk as fast or slow as you want to, but don't stop and don't turn off the road."

"Or we'll ride ye down and give ye a spankin'," rumbled Brian with a look of dark menace. "Ye savvy?"

"Y-y-yes—"

"Thin move!"

The oldster gulped and hastily started for the road.

We stood there watching as he began the long slow trek up the grade. When he'd gone a quarter of a mile Brian and me went to the ranch house. We'd planned to split and go in front and back at the same time, but it wasn't necessary. Lurching sleepily from the back door came Fisher himself, rubbing his eyes and yawning, completely unaware of us standing there. He shuffled towards the well carrying a bucket. He was a sight to see, wearing a red silk robe with naked dancing girls embroidered all over it and funny-looking gold slippers with the toes all curled up.

We let him draw the bucket of water and turn to start back for the house. Then he saw us and dropped the bucket with a cry of alarm, heedless of the water splashing his robe and slippers.

"You—you startled me," gasped Fisher. "I . . . I didn't hear you fellows ride up."

"We didn't," I said. "We wanted to give you a nice surprise."

Brian chuckled, a grating sound like rocks being crushed together. "Aye. A surprise party, Mister Fisher. Just for ye."

Fisher backed a step, jerked his head around uneasily.

"You're drunk!" he said.

"That's not a very nice thing to say," I said sadly. "And if you're looking for the old man he's taking a walk to town."

Fisher spun to look, then spun back, the alarm flaring in his bulging eyes. "I—I don't understand. You—"

"You will, brother."

"But—" Fisher peered at Brian sharply. "I know you! You're O'Brian! You're Saber hands! So that's it!"

"That's what, brother?" I signaled Brian and we moved in on Fisher slowly. He backed away, shaking his head and holding out a palm desperately.

"Wait, you're making a mistake!"

"Mistake was yours, brother. You made it the day you decided Colonel Belknap was a goose primed to lay golden eggs."

Fisher's back hit the house and stopped him. He licked his dry lips, stiffened and sneered defiantly, "You—you don't dare touch me and you know it."

"Don't we, little peacock?" purred Brian, his great hands flexing. "And why not?"

"You know why!" cried Fisher wildly. "The Colonel knows! You keep away! If anything happens to me, he'll hang!"

If my face hadn't been so beat up Fisher would have had to see my reaction to that. I nearly choked as it was, holding my voice under control.

"But who's going to know what happened to you?" I asked softly. "We're magicians, Brian and me. We're going to make you go poof." I snapped my fingers and Fisher jumped a foot. "Here today, but tomorrow, nobody knows."

"Nobody except a few buzzards," snickered Brian. "And 'tis little talkin' they'll do."

Fisher's head rolled from side to side, spittle trickling from the corner of his mouth.

"Just as bad," he squeaked. "If I disappear . . . be same thing—"

"You're lying," I snarled. "You're lying to save your rotten neck!"

"No. I swear! It's true! If I don't show up in Concho . . . once every week . . . books go to Army—"

Right then we found out what a big mistake we'd made by not searching the house.

"Boom! Boom! Boom! Boom!" The ear-splitting explosions came with shocking rapidity from the back door where a frowsy-haired girl stood holding a big twelve-shot Brevete harmonica pistol in both hands, firing as fast as she could work the trigger. She had both eyes tight shut and was screeching at the top of her lungs, "Murderers! Murderers! I'll kill you! I'll kill you!"

She did her dead-level best, coming near to scaring us to death—that was for sure. You'd think with her having her eyes closed she couldn't have hit an elephant, but that she-devil put slugs in me and Brian both! I took one in my calf that spilled me on my face while Brian took one in his thigh and another that folded him in the middle—and dropped him into the dust with a choked moan.

Lucky for us Fisher was as nearly surprised as we were when the girl opened fire. He dropped flat and huddled tight up against the house, and he wasn't being no coward neither. The way she was throwing bullets around it was no place for friend or foe.

When she finally emptied that dammed artillery piece she kept right on snapping it. The noise probably busted her ear drums so she didn't know the gun had stopped going off.

Brian had dropped his Walker Colt when he fell, and Fisher was crawling for it when I recovered enough to lean over and rap my gun barrel behind his ear. He went to sleep peacefully.

John came on the dead run when he heard the shots, but

before he could reach the girl she dropped the empty pistol, pulled her wrapper tight around her in a silly kind of dignity, then passed out cold in the doorway. John paused to see if she was hurt.

I crawled to Brian and rolled the big ox over on his back to see how bad he was hurt. The thigh wound wasn't serious, a clean hole through the meat not touching the bone. But Brian had his hands knotted, over his middle and was groaning. When I pulled his hands away he gave me a dying-cow look.

"Is . . . is it bad?" he whispered.

I stared at the lead slug that had dented and partly pierced the Irishman's big silver belt buckle. I shook my head sadly.

"How do you feel, bucko?"

"Kind of numb."

I nodded again. "Shock. I better dig that bullet out before it wears off."

I took out my bowie knife, tossed it aside and muttered, "No, I can get a better grip on the slug with my fingers."

I dug with enthusiasm while Brian arched in popeyed horror, howling, "No! Stop! Ye heathen butcher!!! Ohhhh, ye cold-blooded savage, ye heartless—"

"Aw, shut up," I snapped. I flipped the mashed bullet on his chest. "You big faker. Get your leg tied up. We've got to move fast."

I wound a bandanna around my calf and helped John tie Fisher on a hoss while Brian was putting a makeshift bandage on his thigh. Neither one of us was going to be running any foot races for a few days, but we managed to hobble enough to reach our hosses.

Of course John had to worry about the girl, but we talked hard and fast and convinced him that she'd be all right. By the smell of sour mash that she gave off her only problem was going to be a hangover. I noticed Fisher had the same kind of smell. I hoped they had a good party, it would be the last one Fisher would have for a long time if our plans worked out.

XVII

WHEN MARK FISHER began groaning and moaning, John had to stop and untie him so he could ride the saddle with his butt instead of his belly. You might think that he would have felt grateful, but the first string of words he used didn't have nothing to do with gratitude.

John winced and said, "Stop that kind of talk or I'll put you back like you were."

Fisher looked his hate but shut off the profanity. If you've ever ridden face down across the saddle you'll easy understand why he mightily preferred sitting up. He didn't stop talking, however. At first it was mostly threats and stuff, for listening to us, he'd realized that we weren't from Belknap and that gave his courage a big boost. With John there he knew he wasn't going to get hurt so he could talk as big and mean as he wanted to.

"What are you trying to pull, anyway?" he demanded after a stop for breath. "What was the big idea saying you were Saber men?"

"We didn't say it. You did," I said.

"Ye said a lot of things, Mister Fisher," said Brian, shifting his position in the saddle to give his aching thigh some relief.

Fisher's eyes widened in alarm at that. You could see him trying to remember exactly what he'd blurted out to us. He swallowed and licked his lips a time or two.

"What . . . what do you mean? What things? I . . . I didn't say a damm—" He stopped, swallowed it, went on, "A thing! I couldn't! There's nothing I could have—well look, fellows, I've never done anything to you, have I?"

Fisher forced a kind of smile and looked at each of us, his voice getting a pleading note to it.

"Of course not," he finally answered himself. "I'm just a simple easygoing man. I don't bother nobody and nobody bothers me. You've made a big mistake about me, you know? Sure, that's it! You fellows are after something and you think maybe I know something about it, huh? That's what it is, isn't it?" Fisher gave us each a hopeful little grin.

"Sure, well, you don't have to get tough with me, fellows! Why, hell, you just tell me what you want, and if I can help I sure will, you know that! I'm always ready to give the other fellow a helping hand. That's the kind of gent I am! . . ."

It was pitiful, the way he kept looking from one to the other of us with that sick grin pasted on his face. I half expected him to start wagging his tail allasame a puppy begging you to like him. Fisher kept it up; even after he was told to shut up he kept trying until behind John's back

I showed Fisher the loaded end of a quirt along with a gesture that he seemed to understand. Least he shut up and rode in a sullen silence for a while.

We were getting pretty near the Quincannon ranch when we pulled up to let the hosses blow. Fisher lifted his head to eye us bitterly.

"All right," he said suddenly. "How much?"

John glanced at him puzzledly. "What?"

"I said how much, damm you! How much does it cost me to get turned loose? Let's get this over with!"

"We don't want your money, Mr. Fisher. And please stop—"

"Horse shit! Not much you don't!" Fisher sneered. "The good Reverend Niles! The wonderful Reverend John!" He spat scornfully. "I always did think you were too dammed good to be true."

"You better shut that big mouth and keep it shut, Fisher," I warned him, watching the expression on my brother's face uneasily.

"Aw, go to hell," retorted Fisher. "I may have to buy my way out of this, but I'll be goddammed if I have to listen to a lot of sanctimonious horse shit from a hypocritical fak—"

Whap!

John's slap caught Fisher squarely across the mouth and sent him spinning out of the saddle. John hit the ground the same time he did and yanked him to his feet, fist drawn back to really smash him good. Then you could see John's iron self-control grab hold and with a terrible effort he let go of Fisher and dropped his fist.

"That was wrong," John muttered. "A wicked thing to do and I'm sorry."

I growled, "He was warned, John. And he sure provoked you."

"That's no excuse!" replied John sharply, helping the dazed Fisher back on his hoss. "I'm a grown man and a grown man doesn't let his temper lead him by the nose into wrongdoing!"

John mounted and scowled at me. I didn't mind, I knew he was mad at himself, not me. "Emotion is a fine spur, Frank, but a man's a fool to hand it the reins!"

Not knowing how to stop him when he got like this I gave him a nod and said soothingly, "Sure, John. Sure."

He glared at me. "It's like putting your eyes out just when you need to see most!"

I nodded and opened my mouth but John wheeled his mount and started off at a fast trot. I glanced at Fisher. He was blinking and holding the saddle horn but otherwise all right. He mumbled something about money, and the rest of the way to Quincannon's was spent trying to make Fisher savvy that he was in a jam that money couldn't buy him out of. I tried, but I don't think I was successful. I've noticed that when once a man's willing to do anything for money, he starts thinking that he can buy anything for money.

Quincannon's was a real hoss ranch. A working ranch I mean. Nothing fancy like Fisher's place, no heartbreaking blue-blooded temptations dancing around giving you liquid-eyed promises of flashing speed and feather-bed riding. The stock in Quincannon's big pasture was pure mustang, wild hosses run down and trapped in the mountains that lay all around the place. Mean shaggy little wicked-eyed beasts, they were enough to make a cowboy's rump ache just to look at them. The lump-headed brutes would be hell to break, pure jolting misery to ride and no speed-burners, but they'd give you all they had and never say no.

The riders who were driving a bunch of the mustangs into a corral by the big stone house were a match for their mounts. Tall, shaggy-haired, they were leaned down to wire muscles and bone, burnt black from constant sun and wind. With their piercing eyes and long hard-jawed faces dusted with powdery alkali they were men to ride far around if you were an enemy.

How they'd act to strangers riding up I didn't know, but when they saw John they acted like a bunch of kids getting a look at Santa Claus. Whooping and yelling they ran to the house and beat on the wall, hollering in the windows.

"Hey! Hey! Hey! Reverend John's ridin' in!"

"Ootside ye lazy Quincannons! The Reverend's coom!"

Out they poured. Everything from gangly-legged pig-tailed girls with bright laughing eyes down to a chubby little toddler whose unsteady legs threatened to spill him on his face and would have but for the quick hand of a handsome girl in blue gingham. There was a mob of them. Following the younguns came several grown women with the heat of the kitchen flushing their faces and their arms floured to the elbow, for this was baking day at the Quincannons. The oldest, a small, round-bodied woman of fifty, stopped at the edge of the long porch. She stood there with her arms akimbo, smiling a warm welcome, amused at the antics of her wild brood.

John spurred on ahead to meet them and was swarmed under. Hands pulled him from the saddle and the young ones promptly started climbing all over him. Watching John swinging the squealing girls high in the air and ruffling the boys' tousled heads, laughing and delighting in the sticky-handed tots that were screeching in his ears and fighting for the place of honor straddling his shoulders, I had a flash of understanding of my brother's power. It wasn't nothing mysterious. He simply loved people. I mean he really loved them, every dirty-faced brat, every sour-faced oldster, all of them. I guess that was John's real religion. He was doing his best to love people into heaven.

Maybe that don't sound very preacherish. You know how preachers are usually whaling away at you about how awful you are and how you're stuffed full of sins and evil and clawing at you to do this and that, pray this prayer, repeat after me, don't do that, bow your head, sprinkle yourself with this, dip yourself in that, light seventeen candles and if you only light sixteen it's hell for you and don't forget to put some money in the box and come back next week.

Nuts! For my dough most churches spend most of their time making religion so complicated their own preachers can't understand it, much less ordinary thickheads like me. They're like a bunch of cooks starting off with a good, simple recipe only none of them can resist adding a bit of this and a smidgen of that and the result is a holy mess.

XVIII

ITT TOOK OLD Cadmus Quincannon to quiet the mob and start things to happening. When he began roaring orders, standing spraddle-legged on the porch like one of those old pirate captains, Quincannons of all sizes and sexes began jumping to obey.

First off, of course, was the problem of getting Fisher put away someplace safe and where he wasn't likely to be seen by anyone. Cadmus solved that one easy, ordering his two oldest sons, Douglas and Duncan, to cart the unhappy Mister Fisher to Cousin Locheil's ranch and there install him in the root cellar. He was to be fed, made comfortable—on John's insistence, naturally—and guarded with care, making sure that nobody saw him or heard him or found out that he was alive. John was gambling on the Quincannons themselves, but he was sure none of them would talk out of turn. After hearing Cadmus warning them I figured John was right.

Not having heard John's arrangements for him, Fisher went into a panic when the two grim young dark-faced Scots started off with him. Fisher squalled in terror, tried to fight his way clear, saw that was hopeless and sat down in the dirt, limp-legged and refusing to move. He reminded me of a spoiled kid. The two Quincannons wasted no words on him. They looked at each other, shrugged shoulders that were ax-handle wide and, leaning down, scooped Fisher up. They toted him to his hoss like he was a sack of potatoes, paying no attention to his kicking and yelling. They tossed him into the saddle and he threw himself right off and lay on the ground screaming that he wasn't going with them.

Duncan—or maybe it was Douglas, they were as much alike as two peas in a pod—unhooked the rope from his saddle and dropped a noose around Fisher's neck. He cinched it snug and swung up on his own mustang. I never saw a man move faster than Fisher did scrambling to his feet and climbing into his kak. With one of the Quincannons ahead and the other behind they headed off up the grassy slope. Cadmus' ranch lay in a kind of narrow strip of land that lay between bluffs rising three or four hundred feet almost straight up. Behind, the land spread out and sloped up for maybe two or three miles before breaking up into steep wooded ridges and long narrow valleys that were gouged into the sides of the mountain peaks themselves. It was rugged country and with Cadmus' place laying like the stopper in a bottle it was easy to see why even Saber avoided moving in on the Quincannons.

What land they had simply wasn't worth the bloodshed it would cost to take it from those wild Highlanders.

Once Fisher had been taken care of, us wounded heroes were next. My leg was sore and aching, but when Brian dismounted and tried to put weight on his leg the big moose turned white and passed out like a light. His wound had gotten all swollen and inflamed. John and Cadmus and two others managed to wrestle the big Irishman into the house and onto a bed, while the women rushed to the kitchen and started gathering up medicines and bandages and hot water.

John took off my boot, poured out the blood and set it by the stove to dry while he fixed the gash in my calf. Me, I sat back comfortable with a mug of coffee with a dollop of good Scottish dew in it and enjoyed the squabble that started between Kate-Ellen, the oldest daughter, and two of her sisters. They were big strapping girls and no prize winners for looks, but not homely neither. The whole thing seemed to be that Kate-Ellen wanted to doctor Brian herself, and the other girls were putting up a big protest.

"I'm the oldest," said Kate-Ellen, who was eighteen.

"I saw him first!" stated Peggy, who was sixteen.

"It's my right!" claimed Kate-Ellen.

"It's not either!" said Mary Lee. "We all should do it!"

"Be quiet!" snapped Peg. "You're too young!"

Kate-Ellen said, "You're both too young! Aren't they, Ma?"

"I'm only two years younger than you are, Kate-Ellen!" Peg replied angrily.

"Three!"

"Two and a half!"

Mrs. Quincannon, who was dumpy and a head shorter than her daughters, was at the stove stirring something that smelled fine. She gave the girls a stern look that was offset by a twinkle in her gray eyes.

"Would you let the poor bogtrotter die while you cackle at each other like geese? Move now, all of you!"

"But Ma!" wailed Kate-Ellen.

"Ma me no Ma's, Kate-Ellen!" snapped her mother. "Time enough for you to be getting ideas about a man after he's got the fever out of his head. Off with you!"

The girls left and a good thing it was, for just then John poured something on my wound that brought me up out of the chair spewing coffee, good whiskey and bad language all over the kitchen. Holding my knee and hopping on the other foot, I howled and fumed and glared at my brother, who was putting the cork back into a brown bottle, eying me rebukingly.

"It's only carbolic acid," he said. "Stop that and sit down so I can finish bandaging you."

He got me back into the chair and put some salve on my leg that calmed down the volcano he'd set off. I looked at Mrs. Quincannon and mumbled that I was sorry for the language and spilled coffee. She wiped it up and frowned at me. "I've heard worse, lad, but you should be more considerate of Reverend John."

I had no decent answer for that. She wouldn't have heard me if I had, for right then there came an outraged bellow that rattled every door in the house. On the heels of it Kate-Ellen, Peg and Mary Lee came flying into the kitchen white-faced and popeyed, all three of them chattering at once.

Mrs. Quincannon and John finally calmed the girls down and found out what happened. It was about what you'd expect. When Brian came to and found three girls trying to pull his pants down he'd thrown a wild Irish fit.

I decided I'd be no help handling the girls so I picked up the carbolic and salve and limped out to see what I could do for Brian. I found his door locked but finally talked him into opening it. He peeked out and around suspiciously, let me in and quick shot the bolt before hobbling back to bed.

"Frank, amigo, ye'd nivir believe what happened!" he started, his greedy Irish eyes on the bottle.

"Sure, I would," I said. "Pull down your pants."

Brian sat bolt upright. "Now don't *ye* be startin'—"

"Aw, for the love of mud, all I want to do is fix that bullet hole in your leg, you big knothead! Now lie down and get those blasted pants off and stop acting like a scared virgin."

Brian blinked at me, scowled and obeyed reluctantly. "Ye don't need to yell at me. 'Tis a sick man I am . . ." When I picked up the bottle and started opening it, he paused to lick his lips thirstily. "But thank the blessed saints that there's a friend like ye to be bringin' a man some real comfort—*Holy Mither, ye've set me on fire!*"

I judged the amount I'd poured into his wound, added another dollop and screwed the cap back on the bottle.

"Quiet, you big baby," I said. "And stop that thrashing around so I can finish treating that little scratch. I had the same thing poured on my leg and it didn't bother me a bit."

Brian answered me at length, but I won't bother repeating it. I was ashamed of the big fellow. He acted very childish about the whole thing. Somehow I got his leg bandaged and pacified him by smuggling in a cupful of Quincannon's liquor. With that warming his insides, his leg bandaged, his modesty protected by two blankets tucked around him tightly, Brian was content. At least I thought he was, but when I was leaving he stopped me and after hesitating and stammering all around Kelly's barn he got out, "Uh . . . oh, by-the-by, Frank, uh . . . about those colleens . . . ye know—"

"Know what?"

"No, no, I didn't mean . . . that is, uh, what I mean is . . . one of thim—"

"Which one?"

"The pretty one, ye know—" From Brian's tone there had only been one of the girls worth looking at.

"That's Mary Lee, she's only fourteen—"

"No, no, no, have ye no eyes? The tall one—"

"What about her?"

I could have sworn a red flush was creeping up to join the greens and yellows and purples that made up Brian's lumpy face. He doubled a fist and said, "Is she havin' a name?"

"Sure. Kate-Ellen."

"Kate-Ellen," Brian repeated and sank back into the pillows.

"She's also got a father, three uncles, four grown brothers and nine male cousins," I mentioned.

Brian didn't seem to hear me. He was looking at the opposite wall like it was a window to heaven. All I could see on the wall were a couple of pair of dirty overalls hanging from nails and a colored lithograph that had been cut from a brewery calendar of some mallards landing on a pond.

Oh, well. I shrugged and limped out to see if I could find another jug of that Scottish dew lying around. I was a wounded man, myself.

XIX

WHEN JOHN finally had time to talk to Cadmus Quincannon, he got a real jolt. Cadmus listened to everything John had to say, then when John asked him to be a candidate for sheriff, the old Scot shook his grizzled head in emphatic negative and refused flatly to consider it.

John couldn't hide his bitter disappointment. "But listen—"

Cadmus' eyebrows—which looked like two handfuls of hay somebody had plastered over his deep-socketed eyes—drew together in a darkly threatening scowl.

"Nae, sir, I willna listen to another word!" he growled.

"But at least give me a reason—" pleaded John.

"Nae!" Cadmus jumped up and pounded the table with a great knotty fist, making the dishes jump and rattle. "I hae gi' ye ma answer, and that's the end of it! D'ye ken me, noo?"

John stood up slowly, his eyes burning at Cadmus, who for all his roaring and table-pounding would not meet John's gaze.

"Yes," John said slowly. "I understand that you're ashamed of something. What is it, Cadmus?"

Well, that nearly did it. I thought the old Scot was going to go right through the roof. He hollered and glared and raved and stomped around the room waving his fist at John. I'll admit I got pretty much on edge, not knowing but what Cadmus was going to try slugging John with something besides noise. It was Mrs. Quincannon who finally put a stop to the furor.

She came from the next room where she and the oldest girls had been chewing moccasins soft while they sewed and stitched and darned on various items of Quincannon clothing. Taking the moccasin from her mouth Mrs. Quincannon stepped between John and her husband, facing Cadmus, stopping him in the middle of his tirade about John being a fool loose-tongued, long-nosed buttinsky who was no longer welcome in the Quincannon home and never would be for ten thousand years, maybe longer—

"You've said enough," said Mrs. Quincannon. "Too much."

Cadmus glared at her in amazement. "Back to your needle, woman!" he barked. "Stay oot of the affairs of men—"

"I'll not! This is my home, too, Cadmus, and the—"

"Woman!" boomed Cadmus.

"And Reverend John will be welcome here," continued his wife firmly, "as long as I'm living in this house. Besides—"

"*Woman!*" thundered Cadmus. "*Leave us!*"

"*Mon!*" his wife suddenly thundered back. "*I will not!*"

Cadmus looked like he'd been kicked in the belly. He wilted, backing a step when his wife moved close, fists on hips. Even on her toes her face was barely up to his gray-flecked beard. But it was too close for Cadmus, the way he backed off.

"Noo, Annie," he said.

"Don't you Annie me! You be beggin' the preacher's pardon and tell him the truth or by heaven, I will, Cadmus Quincannon!"

Cadmus swallowed and looked sick. "But, Annie, ye canna expect me to—"

His wife made a short scornful noise and wheeled to face John. "You were right, of course, Reverend John. This greedy lout of a husband of mine has made a bargain with the devil."

"Noo, Annie, ye shut oop!" said Cadmus, but it was a feeble protest and she ignored it and him. He sat down sulkily and reached for his jug.

"You've been told that Colonel Belknap and that soft-voiced murdering Overstreet have men searching all over Concho Basin for you?"

John shook his head, giving me a look, then looked back at Mrs. Quincannon quickly.

"No," he said, "we hadn't heard."

"Well, it's true, lad. Belknap has heard of your talk of a new election for sheriff."

I couldn't help it. I let out a groan. John frowned at me, then said to Mrs. Quincannon, "He had to hear it some-time. I suppose he was pretty angry about it?"

She threw up her hands. "The man was livid! He was like a crazy man. Yelling about you doing something to Blanche Maginnis and stopping him from getting married and turning people against him, oh and all kinds of things."

She shook her head and the twinkle came into her eyes. "You've upset him, Reverend John. He does not like you."

"I suspected as much," said John dryly.

Mrs. Quincannon looked at her husband and the light went out of her eyes fast. "Well, Cadmus?"

Cadmus emptied his cup and let out a sigh clear down to his boots. "Aye," he said. " 'Twas like this, Reverend . . ."

It took Quincannon a half hour to tell it, what with him stopping every few words to look at his wife unhappily, sigh, and go on. For years Cadmus had coveted the choice piece of land lying next to his and out from the mountains. Several times he'd tried to move onto the land only to have Saber drive him back. Yesterday Colonel Belknap had offered Cadmus the land in exchange for his promise that neither he nor any of his clansmen would accept John's invitation to be candidate for sheriff. Cadmus had hated the idea of doing business with Belknap but the temptation was too much for him. He'd struck the bargain.

"Bargain!" Mrs. Quincannon said acidly. "As if Colonel Belknap will be keeping his word! Once the trouble's over he'll be chasing us right back where we are and that'll be that!"

Cadmus jumped up and stalked around the room with his big knotty fists doubled and his face as black as a thundercloud. "Aye," he muttered. "Aye, Annie, ye're right. I was a fool, nae doot about that."

He looked at John. "Ye've told me mony's the time that a man canna do business wi' the de'il, but then . . ." He let his words trail off, his big shoulders slumped. "I'm sorry, Reverend John."

John shook his head. "No, Cadmus. You owed me no

obligation to accept the candidacy."

The big Scot spun and glared at him. "Ye're no help to a mon seeking peace, John Niles! The least ye could do is show a bit of temper and denoonce ma wickedness!"

"But I'm not angry," protested John, fighting to control a smile.

"Weel, ye should be!" roared Cadmus. "I've done a sinful thing and been a traitor to boot!"

John choked and gurgled before he could finally straighten his face. He rose and put his hand on the Scot's oak-thick arm.

"Cadmus," he said gently, "God is the only one who can give you peace, not me. If you feel you've done wrong, if you acted against His guidance, then you need His forgiveness, not mine. I'm only a man, don't ask me to judge your acts as wicked or sinful—"

"But, mon, ye're a preacher!"

"Exactly," replied John. "My job is to tell people about God—not to *be* Him."

"Huh?" Cadmus stared at John, trying to digest what he'd said. So did Mrs. Quincannon. I guess I stared myself. Sometimes that brother of mine said things that it took a while to get the whole meaning of.

When John finally took Cadmus off in private I wandered out in back to watch Jamie Quincannon making buckshot. The boy was standing on a rock holding a pan of boiling lead over a dishpan of cold water. He was tilting the pan carefully, watching the drops of lead hit the water with a sizzling splash and bust into tiny beads that sank to the bottom of the dishpan. It took strong wrists and steady nerves to make a good shot, and the boy was an artist, but I was too busy worrying to appreciate his work.

Sinful or not, when Quincannon gave his word to Belknap, he kicked the props clear out from under John's election plans. The few other men in Concho Basin that might have agreed to be a candidate were either non-warriors or not the type to swing a majority vote. Knowing John I didn't spend any time wondering if he'd give up his plans. He was too stubborn for that. So I stewed about who he'd decide on as a replacement for Cadmus. A walking target like Ben Steiner, who'd live maybe an hour after being elected? Or somebody like Brian, who'd pull about six votes and couldn't even walk with that hole in his leg?

But all that was minor. My big worry was twofold. What was happening to Blanche? And what was going to happen to John and me when one of Saber's searching parties found us—as they were sure to do long before we finished John's rounds?

I knew the answer, of course. Knowing it made me want to find a deep dark hole someplace, climb inside and then pull the hole in after us. Or get our hosses and line out as fast as we could throw the hooks to them. Or wave a magic wand and change us into a couple of jaybirds, maybe—that was just as likely as getting John to pull out or give up his fool notion of electing a new sheriff and putting Belknap in jail. That blasted brother of mine! There wasn't no way a man could figure on keeping his-self alive riding with John Niles!

"Weel ye shut oop?"

I blinked and looked around but Jamie was scowling straight at me. He added, "Ye're makin' me ruin ma book-shot, ye big farmer!"

There were some thumb-sized balls of lead in the dishpan. I must have made pretty bad noises to cause the boy's hand to jerk that bad. So I swallowed the farmer insult, gave the boy a muttered apology and limped off to the kitchen to see if I could beg some coffee and a piece of Mrs. Quincannon's fried apricot pie.

For the next two days John was busy christening babies—four—doing funerals—two, which was progress of some kind—marrying Bonnie Mae to her cousin, Malcolm MacInnes, which by the way they looked at each other was likely to lead to more of the same kind of progress, holding a hymn meeting and a prayer meeting, and in between talking privately with those who wanted to.

It was the second evening when John gathered up the young Quincannons and headed up the slope to MacInnes' ranch where they'd plague the newlyweds with songs and dances in return for cookies and sweet-meats and steaming hot chocolate. Young Jamie, the buckshot maker, was also the piper, and he skirled loudly if not beautifully as he strode beside John at the head of the mob of kids. John had the four-year-old Bruce strad-dling his neck, and the twin five-year-olds, Lucy and Luckie, clutching each hand. If John had been playing the pipes he'd have passed for the Pied Piper.

Of the young Quincannons, only the babies and Kate-Ellen—who was established now as Brian's nurse—

stayed behind. The girl wore a contented smile now as she moved around the house, waiting on Brian like he was a king or something instead of an overgrown, unshaven beat-up fighting man who was out of his head and raving with fever.

Besides them there was me, Cadmus and his wife, their four oldest—all boys—Duncan, Douglas, Hugh and Blake, and Cadmus' widowed sister, Laurie. Duncan and Hugh were married but their wives had gone along to help John with the kids. Six men able to fight, Brian being too sick to count.

It was no time for Saber to show up, but that's what happened.

X X

AT FIRST IT WAS Belknap and Overstreet with a pair of hardfaced riders tagging along about ten yards back and another ten out to either side, balancing rifles across their pommels, edgy as a couple of panthers. Overstreet was pointing out tracks to Belknap, who was nodding in satisfaction. It was pretty obvious whose trail they were following.

They stopped about fifty yards from the house, and Cadmus burst out the door and went to meet them, taking great strides, his big fists swinging in determination. For the moment I couldn't figure out what Cadmus was planning, then even when it hit me I couldn't believe the old Scot would be so foolish. I was wrong. His conscience was driving him to make a fatal error.

When he was twenty feet from Belknap the two riflemen began lifting their rifles and Overstreet lifted his palm.

"Far enough, Quincannon. We came for the preacher and his brother—"

"And that traitor, O'Brian!" snapped Belknap harshly.

"Hae ye, noo?" Cadmus stood with his fists on his hips, a wild defiant figure. He was hatless and his hair and beard were ruffled by the evening breeze. His tone was mocking with a bitter searing bite to it. "Weel, ye won't be gettin' them!"

"Oh?" Overstreet shifted a little in the saddle, leaning forward slightly. "And why not, Scotty? We know they're here—"

"The reason is that I've changed ma mind!" roared Cadmus, shaking a fist at them. "D'ye ken that, ye spawn of the de'il!"

"You made a deal!" said Belknap icily.

"Weel, I'm unmakin' it! The deal's off!"

Overstreet shook his head. "You've made a very foolish decision, Sc—"

"Get off ma land, ye murderin' pimp!" Cadmus dropped his hand to his gun. "Off wi' all of ye!" He half drew the gun threateningly.

Overstreet had turned white at Cadmus' insult. Now there was a blur of his right hand, a long-barreled gun boomed, spouting black smoke and lances of yellow-red.

Cadmus staggered back as if hit by a giant club. He went to his knees. The gun in his hand roared, but the bullet only ripped the ground at his feet. He tried to lift the gun, wobbled and fell forward on his face. Overstreet calmly put two more bullets into the fallen Scot, then spun and yelled, "Let's move, Colonel!"

Belknap's black stud reared and lunged after Overstreet at a dead run. The two riflemen closed in behind them, turning to open fire on the house as they rode.

The shooting of Cadmus came as a shock, then I snatched up my Spencer and jumped to the door to open fire. The two riflemen were blocking a shot at Overstreet or Colonel Belknap. I drilled one of the riflemen and sent him spilling from the saddle, but he was able to scramble into the rocks at the base of the bluff. With my fifth shot I hit the second rifleman, and as he started around the bluff following Overstreet and Belknap he was sliding from the saddle in a way that said he was either dead or mighty hard hit, but he was out of sight before he fell.

After Cadmus' body had been brought into the house and put on his bed, Mrs. Quincannon ordered everyone else out and shut the door. When she finally emerged her plain face was calm, though you could see the marks of her grieving. On the bed Cadmus was dressed in his best clothes, his hair combed and his beard trimmed, looking for all the world like he'd simply fallen asleep. His blood-stained bullet-torn clothes were wrapped in the bloody counterpane, which she gave Douglas to burn.

That done, Mrs. Quincannon gathered her sons, Kate-Ellen and Laurie in the parlor. I was there, but I stayed in the background, feeling out of place and wishing mightily that John was there. What did you say to a woman who's just had her husband shot to death? How did you comfort her? I didn't have no answers so I kept my mouth shut, but there was a hard ache in me every time I looked at her.

Actually it was Laurie, Cadmus' sister, who needed the comfort. She clung to Mrs. Quincannon's hand like it was her only hope of salvation and every minute or so she'd bury her face in her hankie and sob so hard it shook her whole body. When she did, Mrs. Quincannon stopped talking and would stroke her hair like she was a child, murmuring, "There now, Laurie, there there . . ."

Strangely, it seemed to soothe the grieving woman and her sobbing would slow and stop. Mrs. Quincannon then continued her talk to the others.

"We have suffered a great loss this day," she said. "And it is proper and fitting that we mourn that loss, for Cadmus Quincannon was a good man and we . . ." She paused, then recovered and went on, "And we loved him. We will miss him. But we will not—"

She stopped and looked at each of her grown sons in turn, then her voice hardened. "We will not," she repeated, "forget how he died, nor why!"

"Nor by whose hand," said Duncan harshly.

Mrs. Quincannon nodded grimly. "Aye," she said. "Blood must be wiped out with blood. From this moment on, every man, woman and bairn in our clan is at war with Saber. A war that will end when every Saber man—and every animal bearing that cursed brand—is destroyed—"

"Good God!" I gasped, unable to restrain myself. I thought I knew something about hating, but Mrs. Quincannon's cold-blooded declaration turned my backbone to an icicle. "You can't start out killing every—"

Mrs. Quincannon's look hit me like a rock in the face. "Would you have us sit around crying and sucking our thumbs, waiting for Belknap's butchers to murder again at their pleasure?"

I stepped forward reluctantly, wishing again that John was here to handle this thing. I shook my head. "You know how I feel about Belknap, Mrs. Quincannon. There's nothing I want more than to see Belknap and Overstreet both swinging at the end of a rope, but you're talking about killing fifty or sixty people, maybe more, and you can't—"

"Don't listen to him, Ma!" cried Douglas. "We know what you want—"

His mother waved him silent with a curt gesture, her eyes boring into mine.

"Do you not believe in justice, Frank?"

"Sure, but you're talking vengeance—bloody vengeance, not justice!"

"They can mean the same thing—"

"They can not! You've read the Bible, God said that vengeance was His!—not yours!"

I became suddenly aware of what I was saying and gulped hard. What the blazes was wrong with me? I was talking like John for cripes' sake. What did I care if a bunch of wild Highlanders went after Saber? The more they cut down the less there'd be to shoot at John and me. Not only that Belknap still had my girl—well, the girl I wished was my girl—penned up in Doc Holly's house, playing sick to keep from being forced to marry a man she hated. Hell, I ought to have been cheering Mrs. Quincannon on, not arguing against her! But for some reason I couldn't shut off the words. And believe it or not after ten minutes or so I had Mrs. Quincannon nodding slowly and saying:

"You are right, Frank, but it does not matter. They must pay for the murder of Cadmus—"

"That's what the law is for!"

"What law?" sneered Hugh.

"Real law!" I snapped. "The kind of law John's risking his neck to get for Concho Basin!"

"That's a pipe dream and you know it," charged Duncan.

"I'll admit I don't see how it'll work," I said, "but if John believes it will then it will even if it won't!"

"I still say it's a pipe dream."

I shook my head stubbornly. "John don't smoke."

Duncan snorted in disgust. His mother held up her hand.

"Enough of this. When Reverend John gets back we'll talk about this further." She rose. "Until then, there's every reason to expect Saber to return as soon as Colonel Belknap can gather enough men." She glanced at me and I nodded unhappy agreement. They'd be back all right, knowing me and John were there.

"So nobody goes outside unless it's absolutely necessary. I want each of you—you, too, Kate-Ellen—to get a rifle, load it and keep it beside you. You're not to take one step without it."

She turned to her sister-in-law and helped her to rise, adding gently, "You better stay with the wee ones, Laurie. If there's shooting, they'll be frightened."

Quick concern flooded Laurie's soft eyes and she nodded. "Aye, ye're right, Annie. I'll go to them noo." She gathered her skirts and left the room hurriedly, her own grief forgotten in her concern for the children.

XXI

TWENTY MINUTES later Belknap hit us with twenty-five or thirty men—at a guess, two of his searching parties that he'd put together for the raid. Lucky for us all, Hugh was in the hay barn and spotted them coming or their first charge would have been the last. But instead of legging it for the house as fast as he could the fool boy opened fire on them with his battered old Henry. He sure flung the lead into them. The cracking of his rifle was like the sound of a boy running a stick along a picket fence. By the time the Saber force rounded the bluffs and headed for the house, every front window held a waiting rifle.

It was dark so we waited till they were no more than a hundred yards before opening fire. It was a brutal murderous volley. Hosses and men went down in screaming, kicking heaps and the solid blackness of the charging line of riders was torn into pieces by the hail of lead from six repeating rifles—Kate-Ellen and her mother handling their guns as effectively as the rest of us.

Cursing and yanking their terrified mounts around, the attackers split, wavered, then fled back the way they'd come. All the way Hugh was pouring a hellish fire into them from the barn, but when Saber reached the rocky rubble on either side of the narrow entrance Hugh was trapped. Rifles from the corner of the far bluff would have him outlined against the light-colored wall of the right-hand bluff if he made a move toward the house.

Saber settled down to pour a steady fire into the house, two raiders driving slug after slug into the thin walls of the barn. In ten minutes there wasn't a pane of glass left in any of the house's front windows, and at the barn the Henry's spiteful barking had stopped ominously. Maybe Hugh was being smart and playing possum, maybe he'd been hit. I sent off a couple of prayers by express that it wasn't no worse than that.

It strikes me that you might get me wrong, what with me talking like I did to Mrs. Quincannon and now praying and all. Don't you do it though. I wasn't no preacher; I wasn't trying to be, neither. I wasn't even religious, not the way most folks think of it. It was only that—well, only that the kid was out there in the barn all by hisself, maybe dead or gutshot dying, and John wasn't there, and well, dammit, somebody had to ask God to give him a hand.

By the sound of it one of the raiders had a needle gun. Every couple of minutes in the midst of all the whip-cracking of carbines there'd come this booming bellow like somebody had goosed a buffalo and there'd be the ripping whine of the thumb-sized slug lashing through a window and tearing up things inside the house. A couple of times the slug chewed its way through the cabinet where Mrs. Quincannon kept what was left of her English china. Each time afterwards I heard the woman muttering in Gaelic and emptying her .44-40 furiously in a futile attempt to get the man working that needle gun. I asked her afterwards what she'd said, but she claimed she couldn't remember.

Turned out that Hugh was playing it cagey, or leastways he wasn't dead yet. Lucky for us in the house, too, 'cause Saber tried a sneak along the base of the left-hand bluff. There wasn't much in the way of cover but the shadows were dark from our angle and we never seen a thing until Hugh's rifle opened up. He had them outlined against the bluff, and hosed them good with .44 slugs before they gave up and scooted back for safety. Of course when we saw what Hugh was shooting at we all poured lead into them. From the house we were mostly shooting at shadows. I doubt if we did more than burn a few, but it helped convince them the sneak was a bad idea.

Soon as they were back at the corner they poured all hell into the barn. Hugh had stopped shooting so they had to guess at his position. Even so it was hard to see how anything could live through all that blistering barrage. It looked like the barn was being sliced right off its foundations, and there wasn't nothing inside for a man to hide behind except loose hay and that don't stop much.

After that there was a kind of lull in the shooting on both sides. Just occasional shots and every so often the dammed *boom-whine-crash!* of that buffalo gun trying to knock over the house by itself.

I took the chance to strip my cartridge belt and count the shells I had left for my Spencer. It didn't take very long. I only had what was in the gun—four—and one spare tube plus five loose cartridges. Four, seven in the loaded tube, and five. Sixteen shells.

I called over to Mrs. Quincannon, "How are you fixed for Spencer loads?"

By the dim starlight shining through her window I could see her powder-blackened face grin at me.

"There's a case and a half of Spencer, four cases of .44-40 that'll fit Winchesters, Henrys, or Colt handguns, about ten boxes of .22's for Mary Lee's rifle, a couple of hundred rounds made up for Cadmus' old Ballard .50 and enough powder and lead to reload them all with some over, maybe a hundred ten-gauge buckshot shells, two spare Henrys, two Spencers, one Winchester, the Ballard, Mary Lee's .22, half a dozen Colts, and one Cochran monitor pistol that nobody's got nerve enough to shoot, two .41-caliber derringers, an old Kiowa bow and six arrows, and Cadmus' claymore—a real Andrea Ferrara it is, though you'd not appreciate that . . . ." She paused to take a breath, then said, "When we've used that up, we'll start throwing rocks."

She saw something move and threw up her rifle, aiming carefully. She fired, drew back and thumbed a fresh shell into the receiver. I was gaping at her, completely dumb struck. I finally pulled my jaw up and asked her sarcastically what we'd do when we ran out of rocks. She flashed me another dirty-faced grin, looking like an urchin with the black powder ringing her right eye and smeared down the side of her nose.

"Then," she said, "we spit!"

And right then and there I fell plumb in love with that tough little Scotswoman. I had my mouth open to tell her so when from Brian's room there came a crash of something hitting the floor that shook the whole house. Right on the heels of that came Kate-Ellen's scream.

"Something's happened to Brian!" I gasped.

I ran to his room as fast as I could, cussing with every step. I'd grown kind of fond of that ugly mick and if they'd killed him—I flung open the door and stopped in horror, sure that my fear had come true. Kate-Ellen was sitting on the floor rocking back and forth, clutching Brian's head to her breast and moaning like her heart was gonna break. Both of them were soaking wet and there was pieces of broken crockery all over the room.

I swallowed something hard and painful and moved closer. I could hear Kate-Ellen saying over and over, "Brian—oh, Brian, forgive me! Please forgive me!"

I touched her shoulder. "Kate-Ellen—"

She looked up at me and busted out bawling, "Ohhh! Ohhh, Frank, Brian . . . Ohhh! Ohhh!"

For the life of me I couldn't get her to make sense or to let go of Brian's head so I could see if the big ox was dead or what. I suddenly got sore and yelled at her, "For the love of mud, shut up, will you?"

She stopped and blinked wetly at me in surprise.

"That's better," I said. "Now, where's he shot?"

Her cow eyes promptly filled and overflowed again. "He's not," she wailed.

"He's not what?"

"Shot."

"Then what the devil hit him?"

She wailed louder. "The pitcher!"

"The what?"

She waved a hand at the pieces of crockery. "The water pitcher! I . . . he . . . waaaaaa!" She was off again.

"But . . . how in—"

"I did it!" she sobbed. "I did it! He was out of his head . . . I didn't want to! He . . . he . . . grabbed his gun . . . started climbing out the window—he wouldn't listen to me—"

"Yeah, yeah, so . . . ?"

"So I hit him."

I stared at her. "You hit him?"

"With the water pitcher!"

"You mean—"

"On the head."

"All this—just because you had to slug him?"

The cow eyes spilled over like waterfalls. "But now he'll hate me! He'll hate me!" she wailed.

It took all the grace I had but I controlled myself and didn't never hit her. I turned and stalked off, stopping at the door to look back at her savagely.

"You better get him dried off and covered up," I snarled. "He's liable to catch cold laying there in that water without his pants on!"

I got back to the front room just as Douglas reeled away from his window with blood streaking the side of his face. He fell to his knees before I reached him, but a quick examination showed that he'd only been creased. I left Mrs. Quincannon tying strips of her petticoat around his head and got back to my own window in time to drive back another sneaker.

I reloaded and pulled back from the window to roll a

quick smoke. Watching Mrs. Quincannon finish bandaging Douglas' head I realized that the West wasn't won by guns and bullets. It was won by women's underwear. Without women's petticoats for bandaging, so many men would have died the West never would have been won.

In the barn Hugh never really had a chance and he knew it. There were too many ways Saber could close in on him, and after he'd stopped their sneak they went all out to get him. The first thing we knew of it was when a long yellow tongue of flame shot out of the barn loft.

There were yells of angry dismay from the raiders as they saw the fire. We could hear somebody hollering for them to get in the barn and put out the damm fire. A half-dozen dark shapes scurried around trying to obey, but they had no chance. Hugh had made sure of that. The whole loft was ablaze before he finally scooted for the house.

He ran like an antelope, weaving and bent over, and for a minute it looked like he was going to make it. Saber's guns were putting up a terrific hail of fire but he ran on untouched. From the house we fired our guns as fast as we could work levers and triggers, not trying to hit anything, simply pouring as much lead as we could into the raiders' positions trying to throw off their aim.

It was about a hundred yards to the house and Hugh made half of it before he suddenly stumbled and pitched headlong. I don't know if he was hit then or stumbled, but he scrambled right up and came on, still running fast.

He made another ten yards, twenty, thirty—then it seemed like all of a sudden Saber's rifles found the range on him. He was hit, lurched, recovered, took two steps and was hit again, then again in rapid succession. His rifle flew from his grasp, he cried out hoarsely in pain. He spun, fell to one knee, pushed up, fell back to his knees, his head bowed. He looked like a man praying—maybe he was—then even over the racket of gunfire we could hear the meaty slap of bullets hitting him. He crumpled slowly into the dirt like his bones were all melting inside him.

"Hughie! *Hughie!*"

It was Mrs. Quincannon's voice lifting in an agonized scream. I heard scuffling and turned to see Douglas and Duncan pulling the struggling woman away from the door. I put down my rifle and got up.

"Hold on to her," I said. "I'll bring him in."

The big hero, me. The big lunatic! There were times when I felt like giving up on myself and that was one of them. I knew that Hugh was done for. He must have taken a dozen bullets. There just wasn't no sense at all in a live man going out there to haul in a dead one, yet I had to do it. Like I said, there's times when I didn't have sense enough to pound sand down a rathole.

Which is why I didn't get killed, I suppose. Saber knew Hugh was finished so they didn't expect nobody to be crazy enough to come charging out of the house to rescue him. I'd gotten to Hugh and had him over my shoulder and was starting back before they fired one shot. Packing a hundred and sixty or so pounds I didn't exactly run but I sure wobbled as fast as I could wobble.

And being luckier than any ten men deserve I made it clear to the door before they finally nailed me. I felt something slam me where no hero ought to get slammed, then my head blew up and all the lights went out.

XXII

IT WAS, let me tell you, a hell of a place for a hero to get wounded. It was a hell of a place for anybody to get wounded. The only good thing about it was that there was enough spare meat there to keep a bullet from doing any permanent damage. Except to a man's pride—what it did to that was something fierce!

I came to on my face—naturally—feeling like I was swimming through a sea of white taffy with anchors tied to both hands and both feet. There was a bunch of Comanches doing a war dance inside my skull, pounding on war drums and stomping around to the beat of them while I kept begging them to stop before they cracked my head clear open. When the pounding stopped being agony and became a slow steady throbbing I began to make out words being said in a gentle worried voice.

"Frank . . . Frank . . . it's me, John . . ." the voice said. "Frank . . . it's all right, Frank . . . it's all right . . ."

Right away I felt myself relaxing. I stopped trying to swim. John was there, he'd save me, anchors and all. I felt my head being touched—turned—and right away the sea of white taffy disappeared. I blinked, blinked again, then slowly realized that the whiteness was an enormous feather pillow. I'd had my face buried in it. I could see somebody standing next to my bed and started to turn over.

That was a mistake. When I stopped making noises, the voice gurgled suspiciously, then said, "You'd better stay on your stomach, Frank."

I got my head turned a little more and focused on my brother bending over the bed, his hands holding a bowl and spoon.

"How do you feel?" he asked.

"Peachy," I croaked. "What . . . happened? What am I doing in bed?"

John smiled. "You're a wounded hero, don't you remember?"

Hero! I remembered and groaned. John's smile vanished and was replaced by a quick frown.

"Does it hurt bad?"

It did and not just my head either. I reached a hand back and down cautiously until I discovered my aching rump was now a mound of bandages. I looked at John questioningly. He nodded.

"You were hit twice. One slug bounced off your hard head, the other hit you uh—there." He pointed with the spoon. "You were lucky, Frank—"

"Lucky?" I gasped bitterly.

"Very lucky. It's only a flesh wound. And the other shot only grazed your head. Why, you'll be up in no time. Here, try some of this broth."

"I don't want any broth. Tell me what—"

"You'll like this. It's good." John dipped the spoon in the bowl, headed the spoon toward my mouth.

"I'm not hungry. I want to know—"

The spoonful of broth stopped my words. I had to

swallow to keep from choking. "John, put that stuff down and—" My mouth was full again and again I had to swallow.

"Will you stop?"

He would not. He was as bad as an old woman in that respect. If you got hurt the first thing he wanted to do was feed you. Didn't matter if you'd eaten ten minutes before, if you were injured you needed food.

He finally did start to talk while he shoveled the soup into me. I found out that Saber had made one last try in force right after I went down. The Quincannons had held on by the skin of their chins until the rest of the clan—and John, of course—showed up and proceeded to drive Saber off. The clansmen had seen the light of the burning barn and had wasted no time coming to the rescue.

Even in the darkness we'd hurt the raiders plenty. They'd taken away their casualties but from the blood-stains it was guessed that we must have hit at least eight or ten, maybe more. Of course some were merely scratches, but in four places the large blood puddles told of men that were hit hard.

"On our side there was Hugh killed," I mused, "and me and Douglas got scratched." I stopped and threw a side glance at Brian, who was in the bed next to mine. "We got the best of it all right, even counting Brian's headache, which he didn't get from Saber."

Brian lay unmoving and silent, but I saw the crimson tide flushing up his thick neck into his face. John fed me the last of the broth and put the bowl down. He suddenly looked tired and I noticed the traces of powder marks on his face that meant he'd taken a hand in the fighting, too. When his eyes avoided mine I knew my casualty list hadn't been complete.

"Somebody else?" I asked him.

He nodded wearily.

"Hurt bad?"

He nodded again, sighing. "Cadmus' sister . . . Laurie—"

"But she couldn't have been! She was upstairs with the babies!"

"It was a wild bullet, Frank." John swallowed hard and turned away from me. "We found her lying across little Anna's cradle. She—she must have been tucking Anna's blankets when . . . when it . . . hit her."

I'd never heard such a tone in John's voice. It was thick and harsh, choked with emotion.

"Was she . . ."

My brother nodded but kept his head turned away from me. "Back of the head. She didn't know what hit her, thank God for that."

The picture of Mrs. Quincannon stroking her sister-in-law's hair came into my mind and I asked, "John, what about Mrs. Quincannon? I mean, how's she taking it?"

"Not good, Frank. Losing Cadmus, then her son and Laurie, too . . ." John shook his head heavily and then turned slowly to look at me strangely.

"Now what's the matter?" I demanded.

"Mrs. Quincannon told me how you'd talked to her. About vengeance—"

I had to get him off that in a hurry. I busted in fast with,

"Oh, that was just something I ate. I suppose she's all hotted up about wiping Saber off the face of the earth again?"

John looked like he was going to smile, but he didn't.

"No," he said slowly, "she says she wants to see Belknap punished by law."

There was the slightest kind of emphasis on the word "says," so I gave him a frown and asked, "Only you think maybe she means something else?"

"I don't know, Frank. It's possible." He shook it off irritably. "Anyway she's certainly doing all she can to work with me."

"She is? What can she do to help?"

John grinned suddenly. "You may be surprised."

Which of course meant that he figured I would be. I tried to find a more comfortable position, couldn't and gave it up. A feather had worked its way out of the pillow and into my mouth. I tried to spit it out, got rid of it on the third try and scowled at John.

"Okay, so keep your old secrets. Only there's one thing you seem to have forgotten, brother. In order to have an election you gotta have a candidate."

"I have one," John said calmly.

"You have?" I twisted my head further to survey his face carefully. "Which one? Douglas? Duncan?"

"Neither." John's mouth tilted at one corner. "Though they both offered."

"All right, all right, who is it? Not the big moose?" I jerked my head at Brian.

John shook his head. "Mrs. Quincannon."

I felt my jaw drop open and didn't care. I dug a pinky into my ear to clean it out. "Say that again."

"Mrs. Quincannon."

"Joker!"

"No, true."

"But you gotta be joking! Who ever heard of a woman sheriff?"

John shrugged. "Does that matter?"

"You damm r— darn right it matters! She won't pull a vote!"

"You're wrong, Frank."

"Like blazes! Man, this is the Territory! Why, they'd vote for an Apache before they'd let a female become sheriff!"

"That's simply prejudice."

"Call it any fancy name you like. There still ain't gonna be no woman elected sheriff of Concho County!"

"She can do the job."

"So maybe she can," I admitted, remembering Mrs. Quincannon during the fight. "She still won't get no votes."

"She will. She's going to win the election," said John, his jaw setting stubbornly.

That's when I got mad. I argued and yelled at him for an hour. Result: a sore throat, a headache, and a feeling like I was trying to sweep a dry path through a running creek. It couldn't be did. John stayed patient and calm and stubborn, first to last. He wouldn't even argue with me. All he'd say was that Mrs. Quincannon was the candidate and she was going to win.

John finally left the room saying that I needed rest, which was true enough. I ached top and bottom and I was so bushed I couldn't even answer Brian's cracks about when was I going to learn not to argue with Reverend John.

I decided to take a nap. When I woke up I'd be in better shape to tackle John again. That's what I thought anyway. The trouble was that I didn't wake up for nearly twelve hours, and when I did John was gone!

XXIII

WHEN THEY TOLD ME that John had gone on to complete his rounds—a matter of ten days or so—I was fit to be hog-tied and chained down.

"What's the matter with the blockhead?" I yelled at Brian, who was being fed by Kate-Ellen, though there wasn't a thing wrong with his hands. "Doesn't he want to stay alive? The blasted idiot knows that Belknap has fifty men combing the range for him with orders to shoot on sight! Does he think he's invisible or something?"

"Ulg grmph," said Brian around the spoon, not taking his eyes off Kate-Ellen's face.

"The idea!—the very idea of that crazy brother of mine running off without me like that! Dammitall, he knows I've gotta protect him! Who's going to take care of him out there with all those gunnies? Tell me that, will you? Who's going to take care of the soft-headed jackass? Who?"

"Mgh dm frngh," said Brian.

"Nobody, that's who! He's a sitting duck out there with every gunhand on Saber's payroll getting free pot shots at him! While here I am flat on my back—"

"Stmmgk," said Brian.

"All right, on my stomach! I'm in bed, dammit, and I ought to be out there with him! He's got no chance at all by himself and you know it!"

"But you can't ride," said Kate-Ellen. "Not with that wound in your—"

"Never mind the geography," I raved. "I know where I'm wounded! I couldda used a pillow or something!" I pushed myself up to my knees suddenly and started working my way out from under the covers. "I will use a pillow! Maybe I can still catch up to him in time!"

"Oh, no, Frank!" Kate-Ellen cried in alarm, then gasped and turned a red face away quickly.

"Cover yerself, ye indacent lout!" roared Brian in sudden fury.

"I'm looking for my pants!"

"Cover yer ugly nakedness, blast ye! Nivir mind yer pants! Ye've already offended the lady's innocent eyes!"

I pulled the blanket around me and glared at him bitterly. Lady's innocent eyes, my foot! With four grown brothers how could she be shocked by seeing a man in long johns? I decided, however, that it wasn't a subject I better argue about with Brian, so I clamped my mouth shut and went on searching for my pants.

No pants. No shirt. Not even my boots or hat. After a few minutes of painful lurching around the room I stopped and looked at Kate-Ellen.

"Okay, so where are they?"

She looked blank. "What?"

"My duds! Where'd you put them?"

"Oh." She shook her head. "John gave them to Ma to put away."

"Put away where? Go get them!"

"But I can't! Ma said—"

"You tell your Ma that I want my pants and I want them now!"

Kate-Ellen looked frightened and moved closer to Brian. She shook her head. "I can't, Frank."

"Can't? Why can't you?"

"Ma's not here."

I groaned in exasperation. "Well, go get her! Do something, only get me some clothes!"

"But she's not here."

What a bubble brain! I held my temper with great effort and only snarled, "Having eyes, I know she's not here. Will you please go and—"

"No, no, I mean she's gone. Cousin Angus is driving her to other ranches to talk to some people."

I stared at her bitterly. "Did she," I asked, "take my pants with her?"

Kate-Ellen giggled nervously. "No, of course not—"

"Then get them and bring them here!" I bellowed.

She must have jumped two feet. She scurried to the door, stopped and protested, "But Frank, they have a big hole in the—"

"Get them!"

She vanished. Brian was glaring at me. I glared right

back at him.

"There was no need to be shoutin' at her," he growled.

"How else was I going to get my pants?" I snapped.

"Ye're no gentleman, Frank Niles! Ye disgust me!"

Brian rolled on his side, turning his immense back on me. I felt my patience starting to unravel.

"Oh, for the love of—all I want is my clothes, you dammed billyboat! Is that asking too much? Somebody's got to try and save John's neck—"

The door flew open and Kate-Ellen came back in but not with my pants. With Duncan, Douglas and a burly graybeard that I found out later was another clansman named Callum Evan. Douglas had a bandage over his bullet-ripped ear. They spread out a little, moving towards me with grim smiles.

Duncan said, "Kate-Ellen says that you refuse to stay abed."

I edged back to the bed, groaning desperately. "Aw, look, fellows, you don't understand. My brother's . . ."

They sure as hell didn't understand or even try to. By the time they left I was back in bed with a headache, a throbbing boil-sore rump, and a savage grudge against three thickheaded Scotchmen and a grinning Irish giant that had me mumbling into my pillow for a week.

I swore to myself that if anything happened to John because I couldn't get loose to go help him, I'd skin me some Scotch hides and nail them up to dry!

What with relations between me and everybody being kind of hostile it was several days before I even learned much about what was going on. Not that there was much to learn that was new. Mrs. Quincannon was still away talking to whoever it was she was talking to. She and Duncan had apparently had a fight before she left about who was bossing the clan now that Cadmus was gone. By rights Duncan was the new chief, or as they called it, he was The Quincannon, being as how he was Cadmus' oldest son. But Mrs. Quincannon had flatly stated that until Colonel Belknap and Overstreet were worm food she was The Quincannon and chief of the clan. That may not sound like much reason for a quarrel, but the laws of Highland clans are strict and her taking over command was a revolution and had darned near caused one. When I heard about it I had some second thoughts about her running for sheriff. I still didn't think she had a chance to win any election, but if she did I got the idea that she'd make a pretty tough lawman—uh, lawwoman. However she did it she had the clan behind her solidly now.

There were plenty of reports about Saber riders looking for John, but no further moves were made against the Quincannons. Partly this was on account of the way the main ranch was turned into a regular fort. Most of the clansmen were staying there now and they kept regular lookouts on nearby peaks so Saber had no chance to pull any surprises. Even if Belknap had turned loose his whole army it would have been a bloody job to tackle, and Saber was by no means a cinch to win, odds or no odds. Also, they'd taken some heavy losses in the last fight.

Yet I think what really made Belknap hold off was John. The Colonel couldn't keep a dozen search parties looking for him and still lay siege to the Quincannons. Not even

Saber had that many fighting men. And for sure Belknap's prime desire in life was to rub out the Reverend John Niles. Once that was done Belknap could forget any worries about an election and concentrate on the Quincannons.

I found out that John had taken certain steps to protect himself—besides praying I mean. He'd taken two of the best Quincannon hosses, one of them being Dorchester's Red, a seventeen-hand golden-red sorrel that was all bones and legs and for which Cadmus had given twenty good mustangs plus a fortune in cash to boot. Douglas told me that Mark Fisher had offered double the price for the big red and Cadmus had laughed in his face. Douglas said that John's second mount was a rat-tailed bay mare that was a fit running mate for Red, so that by switching from one to the other there was nothing on four legs that could run John down.

If by some magic any Saber rider did get too close John was carrying a .45-70 that was Douglas' own pet rifle, a hard-hitting gun that would outshoot the ordinary saddle carbine by two hundred yards. I knew how John could shoot, and with a gun like that he'd be hard to get close to—and stay alive, that is. So I relaxed a little, grudgingly admitting that maybe John did have a chance to get back all in one piece.

Besides I still had plenty to worry about. News from town was that Blanche Maginnis was still at Doc Holly's and apparently Belknap still hadn't gotten the doc's okay to move her out to Saber yet. But there were four Saber hands keeping watch on the house as well as Belknap's housekeeper, Mrs. Spain, who'd moved in and was staying there. Blanche's faking could be found out at any moment, or even if it wasn't, Belknap could take it into his head to move Blanche to Saber in spite of Doc Holly's objections. Belknap wouldn't hold off much longer, I knew. I had to get Blanche away somehow, and if she wouldn't leave Concho Basin, I'd bring her to the Quincannons where she'd at least be safe for a while.

Well, maybe I could think of a way to pull off a miracle. I'd seen my brother do it.

XXIV

THEY LET ME have my pants on the day I was able to get up and move around. That was the seventh day after John went out by himself to finish his rounds. Kate-Ellen had sewn a patch on the seat of my pants, and Brian made me admit that it was a darned good job of sewing. I even told her so, which made her turn rosy and lower her big cow eyes modestly. She was the blushingest girl I ever saw.

I still hadn't figured out a miracle to save Blanche.

On the ninth day Mrs. Quincannon returned. She looked a little grim and frayed at the edges, but Cousin Angus was a worn-out wreck. She didn't say much about what she'd been doing, but I gathered that she'd made some kind of whirlwind visit to nearly every rancher in Concho Basin.

John rode in in the morning of the thirteenth day, and he looked like he'd led the charge and retreat of the Light Brigade. Duncan nearly broke down and wept when he saw what was left of the Dorchester Red. The big gorgeous golden-red sorrel was something to shudder at. One of his ears was bullet-torn, hanging lopsided and ragged and crusted over with blackened blood. There was another foot-long gash on his left haunch. His tail and mane were tangled and full of burrs and twigs. He was worn down to skin and bones and was spattered from withers to hocks with dried mud and bloodstains.

John looked about the same. His hat was gone, his jacket was ripped in a couple of places and there was a smear of dried blood on his neck and another one on his hand. He was so exhausted he had to be helped out of the saddle and fell sound asleep walking into the house. He would have fallen on his face except for Douglas' catching him.

The rat-tailed mare was dead, we learned later. A shot from a Saber rider had broken her neck, luckily while John was riding the big red.

It wasn't for nearly ten hours that John woke up enough to talk while he was putting away enough chow for six men. He said that he'd managed to finish his rounds in spite of a half-dozen brushes with Saber. Switching from Red to the mare and back again John had been able to run away from them without any shooting except a few flurries of long-range desperation shots that hadn't hit anything but air.

At night John had camped out, taking no chances on Saber trapping him at one of the ranches. He was on his way back when they ambushed him in a rocky canyon. He fought his way clear but not before they'd killed the mare and come awful close to getting John. He nearly had to ride Big Red to death to escape, but thanks to the sorrel's great heart he finally got clear and made it the rest of the way back to Quincannon's, both him and the hoss going the last few miles on nerve and guts alone.

"How is he?" John paused between bites long enough to ask Duncan worriedly. "Will he be all right?"

"Sure," said Duncan. "We took turns walking him till he cooled off. He ate a little and Jamie made him up a bed of hay. He's sprawled out sleeping like a baby now."

"That's wonderful," said John in great relief. "He saved my life a dozen times, Duncan. It was like riding the wind!"

The lean dark-faced young Scot glowed with his pleasure at the praise of his big sorrel. He fought it down and shrugged broad shoulders. "Red's a good horse," he admitted laconically.

John had some more praise for Douglas' rifle, saying that it was the straightest-shooting, hardest-hitting gun he'd ever used. Douglas looked embarrassed and said, "It's not bad, I reckon."

During all this I caught John casting uneasy looks my way, and I didn't get it at first. Then I realized that he was expecting me to be sore as a boil at him for running off by himself. Which I was, of course, only I'd been so blamed glad to see him back safe and sound—the blood on his hand was from Red's ear and his neck wound was only a nick—that I'd forgotten all about being mad at him.

It came back to me now with a hot rush. I pushed closer to the bed and gave John a black scowl, saying, "If you're all through chatting about hosses and guns, you'd better start making some peace with me, John Niles!"

John blinked sleepily, finished the last bite of pie and put down the plate. "Of course, Frank. Did I do something wrong?"

"Did you do . . ." I drew myself up in furious indignation. "Why, you treacherous, double-dealing, underhanded, sweet-talking, brassbound bundle of—"

Duncan touched my arm and I stopped, then saw that it was no use. No use at all. John's head had fallen back into his pillow and from his half-parted lips came a long soft snore.

My brother John! Some day . . .

John didn't get through with his sleeping until the next night, which was Thursday night. Before he had his boots pulled on I jumped him about doing something to help Blanche out of her predicament.

"Why? What's happened?" he asked in quick alarm, reaching for his trousers.

"I don't know. Nothing, I hope. But it could happen any minute—"

"Oh." John relaxed and smiled. "Well, she's been safe at Doc Holly's for two weeks—"

"Only because Belknap's been too busy to think about her!" I snapped.

"Patience, Frank," said John, standing up to tuck in the tails of his shirt.

"No, sir! I've run clear out of patience and clear out of faith, clear out of everything! Now I'm gonna bust her out of that dammed trap she's in! Are you going to help me or ain't you?"

"Don't curse, Frank," said John mildly.

"Never mind my cussing, answer me!"

"All right, the answer's no! Does that satisfy you?"

It didn't, not by a long shot. I opened up with every argument I could think of, right or wrong, getting louder and madder as I went along. Even John's good disposition began to show a few cracks, but I didn't care. I followed him to the outhouse, sat with him, followed him back, never letting up. He was getting pretty loud himself by this time.

It was a complete waste of time and lung power. John was against the idea to start with, and when I finally gave up he was still against it. There just never was a more stubborn, hardheaded, "I'm again' it" kind of man when he wanted to be than John Russell Niles!

In sheer desperation I made one last try by clamping down on my temper and pleading with him. He gave me a dark scowl and angrily muttered, "That's not fair."

He paced for a minute, then turned and said, "Frank, for the last time, Blanche is safer in bed at Doc Holly's than anyplace else! If we try to rescue her Belknap will know she's faking!"

"Once she's out of there, who cares?"

"If we get her out! Frank, wait! Two more days! Election day is set for Saturday."

"Fine. Let me know if anybody shows up to vote. You still won't help?"

He shook his head and to keep from slugging him I turned on my heel and stalked out. I got my gear and slipped out to the stable, hauled Slug from his comfortable stall and threw a saddle on him. The big gelding had a strong opinion of anyone who'd take him away from this warm oat heaven to make him work for a living. He tried to tromp on my foot, squash me against the wall, gnaw off my arm, and when I reached for the cinch he blew out his belly like a poisoned toad. Which earned him the point of my boot hard enough to empty the air from his gut and start him wheezing and snuffling like an old man with asthma.

It was dark outside, maybe an hour left before moonrise, so I had no problem getting away from the ranch without having to make any explanations. I thought about getting Brian to go with me, but decided against it. His leg was none too good yet, besides he'd have to explain to Kate-Ellen and that would drag the whole Quincannon family into it. I still wished I had John with me, though. I was as cocky as any man about handling my share of a fight, but I didn't have no foolish notions about my brain power. When it came to figuring slick and tricky John had it all over me, and the way I saw it I was going to have to come up with something mighty slick in the way of tricks.

I led Slug on foot for a couple of hundred yards before I tried to mount, and it was a good thing I did. When my butt hit the saddle I was painfully reminded that my wound wasn't completely healed. I let out a squawk and came up in the stirrups, cussing bitterly. Slug decided to join this new game and started a frisky pitching that came near flinging me over his head. I fell forward and wrapped my arms around his neck, hanging on desperately.

"Stop it, you slab-sided hammerhead!" I bawled in Slug's ear. "You . . . miserable . . . crowbait! I said stop it!"

Gambling on losing some fingers I reached around and got hold of the gelding's nose. I dammed near yanked it off before Slug decided I still loved him and settled down to being my faithful slave. He moved off at a gentle walk, ears cocked happily to the stream of blue-smoking comments I was hurling at him. Someday, I swore to myself viciously, I was going to take a gun and blow out his peanut brain.

By trying first one way then another I finally found one position I could ride in. I wasn't comfortable, but at least I didn't feel like screaming every time Slug's hoof hit the ground.

I'd covered about four or five miles when the moon came up big and dollar-bright. Another couple of miles and the moonlight was getting me so edgy I was thinking about leaving the trail and taking to the brush. Then I heard pounding hoofs behind me. They were coming on fast. I hauled Slug around to head for some cover when I recognized the familiar rider. I stared in disbelief.

Either I'd lost some marbles or it was my brother, John.

He came on and pulled up close to me so I could see his slow, easy grin.

"John," I said hotly, "if you think you can make me go back—"

He held up a palm quickly.

"Wrong track, Frank. I thought maybe you could use this."

He handed me a big soft object and be dammed if it

wasn't a pillow! I lowered at him, not sure whether to thank him, or throw it at him. My aching butt won. I slipped the pillow in place, sank down on it with a sigh of relief.

"Thanks, John."

"I'm riding with you, Frank."

"What?"

"You didn't really think I'd let you tackle this thing alone, did you?" John asked.

"Well, yeah, now that you mention it, I did think something like that."

John shook his head and grinned with a flash of white teeth.

"I couldn't do it," he murmured. "Without me you'd be sure to get yourself in a mess, Frank. Somebody had to go along and take care of you, and . . ." He shrugged his shoulders. "I am your brother."

"Why you . . . you . . ." I choked in a sudden fury. "Of all the brassbound gall! You can take your help and—"

I stopped. John had his head cocked to one side and was grinning at me crookedly. The blankety-blank young so-and-so was enjoying himself! I started to really blow up but when I opened my mouth I felt my anger disappearing like wind-blown smoke, and what came out was a laugh. It swelled as I felt a wave of relief surging through me. John joined in and by the time we stopped we were on our way, riding side by side.

Pillow and all, my riding that night was worse than a crippled old woman's. When daylight came we still were six or seven miles from Concho, and I was sagging. I had my teeth clenched so hard my jaw ached, but in spite of this a few groans kept slipping out.

By that time of course we'd left the trail to take advantage of every scrap of cover. John suddenly swerved to head straight into a dense thicket of scrub oak and a thorny bush. His hoss tried to balk but John forced it on and Slug followed like a lamb. Deep in the middle of the thicket John stopped and dismounted.

"Well, come on," he said, "get down."

I shook my head.

"I can't. And if I do I'll never get back up."

John chuckled and came over to help me dismount. "You won't have to. Not till you've had a good rest anyway."

I shoved his hand away.

"What the hell does that mean?"

"It means you're getting out of that saddle and getting some sleep!"

John caught my wrist and pulled. I was yanked off balance and fell right into his arms before I could grab the horn. He ignored my protests, putting me down on some piled leaves. I didn't argue very hard. He had two points and I knew he was right in both of them. First I was in no shape to pull off any rescue with probably some hard riding afterwards. Second, our chances of success being almost nil in daylight, it was far better to wait till dark. So I relaxed and let him talk me into resting during the day and making our try as soon as it was dark. At least, I thought to myself, he didn't notice the cussword I used.

I'd have felt a lot different about it if I'd known what

was going to happen in Concho that day, but not knowing I was content to lay there on those soft leaves on my belly wondering if I ought to take down my pants and see if my wound had opened up. I decided against it, figuring that I was better off not knowing.

John unsaddled the hosses and got them tied so they could browse a little. He broke off a piece of green brush and worked his way back out of the thicket the way we'd come in. I could hear him brushing out our tracks and fixing it so nobody was going to see any sign of us coming into the thicket. The ache in my rear end had eased off to a dull throbbing now. I put my arms under my head and took a long deep smell of the cool leaf mold and the clean woody air, let it out and felt contented. There was a tough problem ahead, but John would figure out some way to lick it. He was a pretty good brother, even if he was a crazy circuit-riding frontier preacher—

"Frank." John was back and hunkering down near me, looking at the beat-up piece of brush in his hands with an unhappy frown. "Frank, I do wish you wouldn't curse so much," he said.

—But he just plain couldn't stand having anybody cuss around him, especially me.

X X V

WHEN I CAME to halfway through the afternoon I felt like something that had been chewed and swallowed and throwed up. It took about all I had to crawl up and join John where he was sitting on a hump of ground a dozen yards in from the edge of the thicket. It was high enough so that he could see a good deal, including a stretch of the trail that ran past a quarter of a mile away.

John looked around at me, gestured in quick sympathy and made room for me to lie down beside him. Times like these he was at his best. He didn't waste a lot of stupid words asking me how I felt and saying gee, that's tough, and all that junk. He just made room for me. When I got settled, he took a piece of jerky from his pocket, tore it in half and handed me the biggest part. It tasted like the inside of a boot but at least chewing it took my mind off my, well, off other things.

We sat there and gnawed away in silence for a few minutes, then I spat out a piece of gristle and asked, "Seen anything?"

"Bunch of riders about ten o'clock, that's all."

I grunted. I tucked the rest of the jerky in my mouth and rolled it around to soften it up enough so I could chew it without busting a tooth. I noticed the look on John's face then and as soon as I could get my mouth clear enough I said, "You worrying about something in particular?"

He nodded. "Fisher."

I jerked my head up and stopped chewing. "Hey, that's right! Do you think something went wrong?"

"I don't know." He shrugged. "He might have been bluffing or we could have guessed wrong about the whole business."

Recalling how Fisher had acted and talked I shook my head emphatically. "Uh-uh. He was blackmailing

Belknap, I'm sure of it, John. Of course he could have been bluffing about what would happen if he disappeared."

John looked sick. "If he was we could be in a lot of trouble."

Thinking of that, for some reason I had a problem swallowing that last mouthful of jerky. But there was no point in sitting around stewing about what might happen if. Besides, I had something else that had been running around in my head and I'd finally come to a decision about it. I made a couple of false starts before I was able to blurt:

"John, I like this country."

My brother glanced at me curiously.

"That's nice," he said.

"I mean . . . well, I like it a lot," I tried again.

"I like it too," he agreed.

I said desperately, "You don't understand. I . . . think it's just right!"

"You do?" John's look became openly quizzical now.

"I sure do! It's, well, it's beautiful and . . . and there's lots of opportunity and . . . and well, everything."

"Everything?"

"Well, you know what I mean."

John smiled faintly. "I'm beginning to."

I shifted quickly to a new point. "I'm not getting any younger, John."

"That's true," said John solemnly. "Then who is?"

"But I'm getting old! I mean—well, you know, I'm thirty—"

"Twenty-nine."

"That's almost thirty!"

"So it is."

I glared at him helplessly. "That's time for a man to settle down someplace and get himself a . . . well, to settle down."

John studied me with a thoughtful frown, then said, "You want to settle down in Concho Basin, is that it?"

I nodded.

"Well?"

"Well, what about my promise to Ma?"

"You know she wouldn't t hold you to that," said John irritably. "Not if you're sure you want—"

"I'm sure!"

"Then stay. Settle here. Can I help? I've got about sixty-five dollars saved up."

"Where the h— where'd you get sixty-five dollars?" I demanded, then flushed. John smiled at me. He knew what I was thinking. As a rule from town to town he collected just about enough hard money to keep us in clothes and me in smoking. The most I ever knew him to have at one time was a ten-dollar gold piece that a rich rancher gave him for marrying off his homely daughter. John didn't keep that for very long. Most of it went to buy medicine for a sick family in the next town.

"It's what's left out of my share of Pa's estate," John explained gently. "I've hung on to it for—well, in case there was some special need, you know."

I knew all right. I also knew that he'd only gotten two hundred all told, and that was three years ago. I'd spent mine in two weeks buying myself a new saddle, a pair of custom-made boots from Mitchell in Waco, and a four-day binge that still made my head ache to remember it.

"Well, you keep hanging on to it," I muttered. "I ain't that special."

John was smiling and starting to shake his head when something on the trail caught his eye. He looked, then with an exclamation he jumped to his feet and ran to his hoss.

He didn't bother with saddle or bridle, just noosed the tie rope around his mustang's nose and went up on him like a panther. He sent the hoss crashing out of the thicket while I spun around and looked to see what had caused all the fuss.

It was plain to see. There on the trail hunched high on the withers of a bony little pinto was a small figure that could be none other than Jim Maginnis. He had the mustang in a pounding gallop and was walloping the pinto's rear with his hat at every jump trying to get more speed out of him.

I felt my blood turning ice-cold. No ranch-bred kid like Jim was going to push a hoss the way he was doing unless he was scared out of his wits. He wasn't no kid to scare easy, either. I started getting a sick kind of hunch and it drove me off the hump to get Slug saddled as quick as I could.

In three minutes John was back with Jim and the boy was chattering away wildly, the words tumbling out of him like popcorn out of an overheated popper. Two minutes of listening to him and I felt the same way.

Cutting it down to the raw facts Blanche had tried to pull a sneak out a back window. Mrs. Spain had caught her in the act and hauled her back, yelling for help. The Saber guards and Doc Holly had come running. They'd locked Blanche in her room and sent a fast messenger with the news to Colonel Belknap. They were expecting him to reach town in a couple of hours, maybe less.

"Oh, that crazy little redhead," I groaned. "Why couldn't she have waited? If she'd only had a little patience—"

John turned and looked at me. I couldn't meet his eye and I felt my face getting hot. Jim looked at me puzzledly.

"What's the matter with him, Reverend John?" the boy asked. "He's gettin' all red in the face."

"So I'm getting red," I grated. "I got the right to get red if I want to, ain't I? You got no learning!"

"I have too! I got lots of learnin'," he said defiantly. "Ma's teached me plenty! More'n you, I bet!"

"Huh!" I sniffed scornfully. I decided to ignore him. There'd be time later to let the kid know who was boss and teach him how to respect his elders.

I heard John make a funny sound but when I jerked around he was innocently studying the western sky.

"About an hour till sundown," he said. "Two and it'll be dark."

Then John did something that made no sense at all. He turned and snatched a slingshot that was sticking out of Jim's hip pocket.

"You any good with this, Jim?"

Jim backed off a pace, eyeing him with the wariness of

a boy that's been hauled on the carpet for more than one broken window. He nodded slowly.

"Yeah," he admitted. "I kin shoot it purty fair."

"Any of the other kids in town have slingshots?"

Jim stared at him puzzledly, still uneasy about what John was getting at.

"Shore," he said. "All of 'em. Whatcha after, Reverend John? I ain't busted nothin' fer weeks—"

John grinned. "Nothing like that, Jim. I've just got an idea how we might help your mother get away from Doc Holly's. Now, you listen good."

John started talking and he talked for ten minutes, laying out his plan and making Jim repeat it to be sure he had everything straight. He sent the boy scooting back to town and began to saddle up while I leaned against a tree and gawked at him in plain amazement.

"You ain't serious," I said finally.

My brother threw me a smile and shrugged. "Why not?"

"Well, because it's crazy, that's why not. It's the craziest thing I ever heard of!"

"It'll work," he said quietly. "And it's better than a lot of shooting and killing." He sighed and shook his head. "You should try and get over your bloodthirsty attitude, Frank. There's always a better way, you simply have to find it."

I mumbled something, shook my head, got my pillow and began the job of getting back on top of Slug. I never have figured out how to talk to crazy people, and from what I'd heard John had gone clear bats at last.

XXVI

DOC HOLLY'S house was a frame cottage stuck in the middle of a bunch of trees and set back from the street fifty feet or so. Five or six rooms, big screened-in porches front and rear. We'd ridden at a slow walk to give Jim time to get his part done, so the sky was graying over fast by the time we reached Concho. When we eased up back of Holly's we found Blanche's blaze-faced chestnut saddled and tied right where it was supposed to be. I mentally tipped my hat to the kid; he was one you could bank on.

We left our hosses and went the rest of the way like scared Injuns. Under the trees it was dark with shadows so we didn't have no trouble till we got to the house. Then we ran into plenty.

The four Saber guards must have been alerted by Blanche's attempt to escape. Jim had told us that they had been on the porches, two in back, two in front. Not so now! There was only one on each porch. The other two were walking circle beats around the house and they were carrying the wickedest hunk of close-range murder man's ever invented, short-barreled shotguns.

We came within an ace of leaving this vale of tears, right about then. John was about six feet ahead of me and to one side and I was about to leave the shadow of a thick tree to move up when directly ahead of me a figure appeared. He was a real pro and not wasting any breath on challenges. I saw him throw up his shotgun, leveling at

John gut-high.

That was a bad moment. There wasn't no way on earth I could have saved John. By the time I got my gun up, even if I beat him to the shot his blast would be certain to nail my brother. But a curious thing happened right then.

There was a soft thumping sound, about what you hear when you thump a watermelon to see if it's ripe. The guard seemed to shake his head, then he swayed and the shotgun drooped. It wasn't much but it was enough time for me to reach him and lay the barrel of my pistol alongside his head with a full-armed swing, folding him up like a wet blanket. As he went down my left hand caught the shotgun just before it hit the ground.

John wheeled around quickly, saw what was happening. He quickstepped over and knelt beside me. I was feeling the Saber man's skull.

"Is he all right?" John whispered.

I nodded. "Don't feel no brains leaking out."

He shuddered at me.

"Frank, please!"

While John carried the guard back into the trees and attended to his future silence I picked up the shotgun and took the guard's place, walking around the house. I'd taken maybe a dozen steps when the second walking guard showed up, moving the opposite way. He lifted a paw at me in recognition and passed on. I let him have two steps then turned and bumped the back of his skull with the shotgun butt. He lost all interest in what was going on.

With him tied and gagged and the other two guards

located on the porches John and I moved to the side window that was Blanche's room according to her son. It was, and we got a real break in that the Saber housekeeper, Mrs. Spain, was out of the room at the time. Blanche was on the bed trussed up like a Christmas goose. Her hair was a mess, her clothes all twisted around slaunchwise, and she was the maddest-looking female I ever saw.

We got the window open with only a little squeal and went over the sill like a couple of eager burglars, one after the other. When Blanche saw us her eyes stuck out and grew round as saucers. She had her mouth open when John bounded to the bed and pushed back with his palm whatever was coming out.

I took out my knife and began slicing her bonds, cussing under my breath when my nerves betrayed me into nicking her wrists. Once she was loose John and I started massaging her legs to get the blood flowing, but she pushed us away and whispered, "I'll do that!"

While the rope-cutting and massaging was going on we could hear voices coming from the other part of the house. It sounded like Doc Holly was plenty unhappy. He was squawking bitterly about Blanche's being tied up and kept a prisoner in his house. He didn't like all the guards around the place, besides which they were rude and dirtied up the kitchen and not only drank all his booze but all of his medical alcohol as well, and when he objected one of them had hit him, and the whole thing was illegal and could get him into a lot of trouble, and so on and so on.

Answering him was obviously Mrs. Spain, who had a

voice like a slice of green grapefruit. Her replies were short and to the point, the same point, all of them.

"Speak to Colonel Belknap," she said.

It was a safe point, and a safer bet, that Holly would never brace the Colonel with any complaints.

We helped Blanche to her feet. She staggered at first, recovered her balance, took a tentative step and nodded that she was all right. John indicated the window. Blanche shook her head in angry stubbornness..

We stared at her in surprise. She was looking around the room. She finally lurched over to a table and snatched up a big graniteware basin.

"Not till I've settled with that . . . that . . . witch," she hissed. "I'm going to ring her head like a gong!"

With that my sweet-tempered redhead started for the door! The nutty girl was going looking for Mrs. Spain! Me and John quickstepped to stop her, but before we took two steps there was a sound outside that froze the three of us where we were.

Through the open window we heard the loud clattering of a big bunch of riders pulling up in front of the house. Colonel Belknap and Saber had arrived! His sharp commands crackled out.

Mrs. Spain's voice came our way: "There's the Colonel, now. I'd better get her ready to go."

Blanche broke for the door. When it opened, she greeted the tall angular woman with a two-handed sweep of the heavy basin that almost knocked her head off.

Whannnggg!

"Tie me up, will you?"

Whannnggg! Whannnggg!

"Pull my hair, will you?"

Whannngg! Whannngg! Whannngg!

Me and John dived for Blanche and yanked her away from the crumpled figure. I made Blanche drop the dented basin and we dragged her swiftly to the window and tossed her out, tumbling out after her as fast as men could tumble.

It wasn't fast enough. Belknap's riders were moving around the house and spotted us almost at once. They yelled and steel flashed in the moonlight as they spurred toward us.

They had us cold. There was no escaping, we couldn't have stopped what was coming with a battery of Gatling guns. Thanks to John, however, we had something better.

It was a funny and eerie thing to watch. There was a dozen or so riders in the bunch bearing down on us. They were no more than fifty feet away when they saw us and half that far when their hosses blew up in the wildest mess of pitching, twisting, sunfishing, screaming confusion I ever hope to see.

I stood there gaping, I'll admit it. It was like seeing some terrible kind of black magic at work. All those well-trained mustangs acting like locoed idiots, squalling and rearing and trying to climb clear up on top of each other, and paying no attention at all to their riders cussing, spurring, yanking and quirting. Several of the riders were tossed head over hip-pockets first crack out of the box, and others followed. Five or six of the riders tried to shoot, but stopped when they saw they were as likely to shoot one of their side as us. In fact it's a wonder they didn't plug themselves the way that tangle was whirling around.

Belknap came charging around the house on his big stud, and the stallion promptly uncorked in such a screaming fury the Colonel was hurled high in the air and landed in some rosebushes next to the house.

I'd have probably stood there gawking until I got a hole blown through me if John and Blanche hadn't hauled me away. We made it to our hosses, swung up and headed out of Concho as fast as my rump could stand it. When we were clear of town and a look back showed Saber was not even on our trail yet, I shook my head and let out about a gallon and a half of breath.

John heard me and I heard him going chuckle, chuckle. Usually when he did that I wanted to throw something at him, but right then I was willing to crown him as king of the mountain and the best all-round miracle-maker that walked in boot leather. Not that I bothered telling him that. All he'd have done was shrug and shake his head and tell me that he couldn't accept the compliment himself, but he'd pass it on to his Boss. John could be awful dog-gone annoying at times.

Of course Blanche didn't know what had happened, so John had to explain to her about his secret weapon and how it happened to be there ready to stop Saber from putting a quick end to the Niles clan. When John finished Blanche threw back her head and laughed fit to bust a corset stay.

"You mean . . . Saber was—that mess back there—was

caused by a bunch of kids with slingshots?" She whooped.

John grinned and nodded "They were hidden up in the trees. I told Jim to have the kids shoot at the horses' noses and flanks, anyplace where the sting would cause them to start bucking. As soon as we'd gotten away they were to scoot for home. Jim went to Effie's, of course." John paused to chuckle. "In the confusion I doubt if Saber ever did know what happened."

"They will," chortled Blanche. "Oh, man they will. And when this story gets around we won't have to fight Saber! They'll be laughed out of the Territory!"

It was pretty gay and happy for an hour or so, but a few minutes after moonrise all the fun went out of life. Blanche's pony stumbled and inside a hundred yards the animal was limping so bad we pulled up and took a look. One match showed the trouble, a sliver of rock buried deep in the tender frog, too deep to get at.

Trying to ride him further would only lame him for good, so we took off the saddle and bridle, cached them in some bushes and turned the pony loose. Blanche got up behind John, him being lighter than me. I tried to argue that Slug was the strongest hoss, but it didn't work.

We started off again, me and John looking at each other, both of us knowing that with his hoss carrying double our lead over Saber was not going to last long. And that big fat shiny moon coming up was robbing us of the safety of darkness.

John suddenly pulled up. "We've got to find a hole."

"In a hurry," I agreed.

Not knowing the country we turned to Blanche, and she tried and finally remembered one place that might serve to hide us, at least till morning, which was John's comment and made no sense to me, but I'd reached the point where he didn't have to make sense. If John had said let's paint ourselves green and play like we're trees I'd have grabbed for the paint brush without a protest.

XXVII

A S A PICKER of hiding places Blanche could have stood some big improvement. Her place turned out to be a cave halfway up a boulder-covered slope. It was big enough to hold the two hosses, and that was about all. The three of us were scrunched up together in the narrow opening, hidden from below and one side but not from the other or above. There wasn't no water, no forage, no warmth, no nothing, not even a soft place to sit except my pillow and I gave that to Blanche. John started to say something about my wounded rear but I gave him a look that made him think again about that.

That was about the worst night I ever spent. It wasn't just that our rocky nest was miserably uncomfortable, or even that every so often we could hear Saber riders passing much too close and had to sit there holding our breaths while we wondered if they'd spot our sign. The real bad thing was Blanche.

She was worn-out and exhausted and between us John and me were able to keep her warm enough so she could sleep a little. I shifted and squirmed and wiggled but every time she dozed off she tilted John's way and wound up with her head on his shoulder. Some of the moonlight glanced off her face and she looked so beautiful it made me ache something fierce. You know how kids look when they sleep? No matter what kind of monsters they are when they're awake, asleep they get that angel look that makes you go all mushy and warm inside. John said once that it's because they look so little and helpless. Maybe so. Blanche was little enough, but it was hard to think of her being helpless, even when she was snoozing. If I hadn't had the stomach of a goat I'd have thought maybe I just had a bellyache. Whatever it was it was something I hadn't felt before. I wasn't even sure I liked it or not.

When Blanche had to leave us for a couple of minutes for a trip behind some boulders, I took it up with John. He was dozing but I punched him awake.

"John. I'm in love."

"That's nice," he mumbled and edged away.

I punched him again.

"No, I mean it. I really am in love."

He opened one eye at me. "With her?"

I nodded miserably.

"I thought maybe it'd go away but it's gotten worse."

John's eye closed, then both opened and he pushed himself to a sitting position, yawned and scratched his chest. He swallowed a couple of times, made a face at the taste in his mouth, looked at me gravely.

"Want the truth?"

"Even if it hurts," I said stoutly, and the way he was acting I was pretty sure it would.

"You're not," said John.

"Not what?"

"In love."

"The hell I'm not!"

"Don't curse. You can't be. Not yet."

"What's the matter, don't you think I know how I feel?"

John nodded. "Of course you do, Frank. The trouble is you don't understand what it *is* you feel."

I thought about that for a moment and said grudgingly, "All right, maybe I don't. I think I do, but you tell me."

"You won't get sore?"

"Of course, I won't get sore!"

"What you're feeling is what every animal feels."

"Wha-a-a-t? Why, of all the dirty, low-minded cracks—"

"Now you're getting sore."

"You damm well betcha I am, only I'm not getting, I am sore! You can't say a thing like that—"

"Frank, you promised!"

I fought a battle with myself and got myself calmed down, at least enough to button my lip so John could explain.

"Try and understand, Frank. People are basically animals and have the same basic needs. That includes the need to reproduce. There's nothing dirty about that, it's simply a fact of life."

"Ain't there any such thing as love?"

"Of course there is. But love is not free, Frank. It's an earned treasure, one that's built on a foundation of strong physical desire and mutual respect. You have the foundation of love now. If Blanche feels the same way then you're ready to start building love."

I growled, "The way you talk it's like I'm starting to build a house."

"That's exactly the way it is, Frank. Two people with the right foundation can build themselves a cottage or a palace, or a mess, it all depends on how much they're willing to give to the day-by-day building. Have you talked to Blanche about how you feel?"

I flushed and shook my head irritably. "When have I—"

Hearing Blanche's footsteps I cut myself short and sat there feeling like a fool schoolboy. I couldn't even look at her when she joined us. After a couple of minutes John cleared his throat a time or two, then got up.

"I better cut some feed for the horses," he said and vanished into the darkness.

There was a long silence.

"Blanche," I said.

"Yes, Frank?"

"I . . . uh, that is, are you comfortable?"

"I'm all right."

More silence.

"Frank?"

I jerked and answered eagerly, "Yeah? Yes, Blanche?"

"Can I ask you something . . . something, well that's kind of personal?"

"Of course you can. Anything." I was having a hard time with my breathing. I edged closer.

"Do you think a woman—a widow—ought to wait a long time before she marries again?"

"No! I mean, well, I don't think so, no. Not if she finds

somebody that . . . well, that she likes a lot. If they got the right kind of foundation it'll work out fine."

Blanche sighed in the darkness. "I'm glad you said that. Of course I'm trying to think about Jim, too. A boy needs a father—"

"Sure, he does," I said. "Especially a swell kid like him."

"Do you like children, Frank?"

I gulped a couple of times and blurted, "I'm crazy about them—that is, I'd be crazy about your kids—"

"John loves them, too," she said. "I can tell."

Before I could answer John came up and threw an armload of forage in to the cave for the hosses, squeezing down inside the entrance quickly, whispering, "Shhhh, riders close."

We sat tensely, listening as riders worked their way past, moving through the boulder field just below us. The butt of my gun was slick with cold sweat against my hand. It seemed like hours before the sound faded away. We relaxed, but there was no chance for me to do any talking with Blanche, and her last remark sat in my brain like a coal that wouldn't burn out.

What had she meant by the comment? Was it just a comment or was she trying to say something about her and John? She'd been warm and friendly, but was that merely because I was his brother, or because I was me? For the rest of that agonizing, never-ending night I hunched there, my mind wiggling around like a worm on a hook. I cussed myself up and down and sideways for being so blamed tongue-tied and awkward. And for being scared to say right out what was on my mind. And for two-three hundred other things. I thought about what she said, remembering every word, the way she sounded, and I took everything apart and peeked under the edges trying to figure exactly what she'd meant as well as what she said. I'd get it all straight in my mind then start arguing with myself and go back and do it all over again and come up with a different answer.

Mister, I was miserable.

It took about twenty years but that night finally did come to an end. The eastern sky grayed over, then all of a sudden the sun was looking over the ragged edge of the distant mountain ridge. John got to his feet with an effort and stretched some of the worst kinks out of his muscles. He slipped off to the top of the slope, from where he could see most of the surrounding country. He took a quick survey and came back trotting.

"Up and at 'em, my brave ones," he grinned at us. "We're going to start moving."

Blanche's left eye fluttered open and regarded him coldly. "You," she said, "are dreaming. Wake up and go back to sleep."

Her eye shut. John laughed at her softly.

"Come on, wake up, wake up, the sun is up! The lark is on the wing!"

Blanche shuddered and snuggled closer to me. "Shoot him, Frank. He's your brother."

"Maybe if we're quiet he'll go away," I muttered.

"Up, you slugabeds! It's election day!" roared John.

Election day, ha! More likely our dying day, I thought. John kept after us and we slowly got ourselves untwisted and unkinked and into the saddle. I could understand that John didn't want Saber to trap us there in that dinky cave, but for the life of me I didn't see that leaving it was going to help any. Even with the hosses rested we couldn't win no races and with my sore butt I wasn't even going to try.

Which was why when we were spotted by a big bunch of riders who started for us in a hurry I figured it was all up with us and headed for the nearest cover to sell what I had for the best price I could get.

That was my intention. John had other notions and he swung back of Slug and rammed the toe of his boot into his flank.

"Ride, Frank! Ride!" he yelled.

I didn't have no choice. Slug nearly went flying out from under me in his reaction to the painful jab. All I could do was to grab leather and hang on, trying not to holler blue murder with every jolt. In ten jolts my rump was on fire, in twenty my wound was busted open and the warm blood started to soak through my pants.

John aimed for the main road that ran out of Concho towards the foothill ranches. When we reached the road he turned on it, spurring like he thought we had some chance of reaching the Quincannon ranch. We didn't. Saber was barely a half mile behind when we hit the road, and they were closing the gap rapidly. But this was one of those times when John always said to have faith, so I gritted my teeth and spurred Slug like I thought we had a chance, too.

The big gray promptly edged up alongside John and Blanche. I was giving John a big jaw-clenched grin to show how my faith was doing, then I saw the pillow. Blanche had one arm locked around John and the other hand was holding the pillow under her rump. I watched her rear bounce on the pillow twice, then decided there was a limit to how gallant a fellow had to be, even with cute little redheads he felt like an animal about. I yelled at her to get her attention.

"Hey! Hey!" I pointed. "Let me have the pillow."

Blanche looked at me puzzledly. She shook her head, not understanding. I edged Slug closer and roared, "Gimme that blasted pillow!"

Not waiting I leaned over and grabbed it out from under her. Letting Slug drift back I shoved the pillow under my seat and groaned out loud in joy. Blanche had her head screwed around watching me with a frown of amazement, but I knew I couldn't get her to understand while we were riding.

By now Saber was no more than three hundred yards back. It wasn't no use—what was?—but I drew my Spencer and threw some .56-caliber discouragement at the pursuers. I must have gotten pretty close with some of the slugs because the front line of riders did some fine and fancy swerving. It cost them a few yards but they came right on again.

In a couple more minutes I started hearing the whine of bullets, but they weren't even trying to shoot close—not with Blanche likely to get hurt. They weren't going to take any chances of hitting Colonel Belknap's "fiancée."

I took my pistol out and got ready. If I left Slug I figured that Blanche could switch over to him, then if I could delay Saber a minute or two, she and John would have a skinny chance of getting away. I didn't want to think about what was going to happen to me, so I got my mind fixed on one idea, getting Belknap. Overstreet, too, if I could, but if I could put one slug in the Colonel's belly I'd be satisfied.

You can easy see that I was fixing to play hero again. It was some kind of sickness that I seemed to get around Blanche. It was going to get me killed dead, too, if I didn't get myself cured of it.

This time I was saved by a surprise. Leastways it was a surprise to me. I reckon it came as a shock to Saber. We were pounding around a bend in the road and I was putting the hooks to Slug, trying to bring him up level with John's hoss to yell over to Blanche for her to get ready to switch to Slug. Then we were right in the middle of the biggest mob of wagons and people I ever did see.

XXVIII

THE WAGONS were mostly buckboards and one or two buggies. The people were ranchers and farmers, each one with a woman beside him, which turned out to be important. They were dressed to the teeth in their Sunday best, shiny serge suits and hard-boiled shirts, dresses that came in every color of the rainbow, hats with feathers, hats with wax fruit, hats with flowers, hats with doodads. Even Piggy Dean was there looking miserable with a stiff collar shutting off his wind.

I recognized a lot of the people as being ranchers John

had talked to. The Quincannons were there in force led by Mrs. Quincannon, all of them in black but with a strange touch added that gave me a funny feeling.

Every one of them had on something that was colored a deep blood red. On Mrs. Quincannon's black silk dress it was a red rose, on the men it was a flower or just a scrap of red cloth pinned to the front of their coat. I noticed that every coat bulged over a holstered gun, and rifles stuck up from saddle scabbards. Leaning on the seat next to Mrs. Quincannon was a double-barreled shotgun.

There must have been a hundred people in that crowd and all of them tried to crowd around John and talk at once. Blanche swung down and joined Mrs. Quincannon, picking up the shotgun, but John leaned over and took it out of her hands with a smiling headshake.

All this time I was yelling my head off about Saber and I got the Quincannons and a few other men up front with rifles out before the Saber riders swept around the bend and came to a skidding, rearing halt that sent a cloud of powdered alkali dusting over the ranchers.

Colonel Belknap and Overstreet pressed towards me and John, and I let the muzzle of my Colt have a good look at them. Overstreet gave me a sad smile and lifted his palm. He hadn't bothered to draw the carbine from his saddle boot. Belknap hadn't drawn his saddle gun either, but he had his naked saber in his gauntleted right hand and in his left was a big Adams revolver.

Belknap's face was flaming under the layer of alkali, and his eyes were sick with his hate. He slowly lifted the saber and used it to point at John, then me.

"You," he said, "and you. Come here."

We didn't move and his face went a shade darker. He seemed to have a hard time swallowing something.

"Did you hear me?"

"We heard you," said John.

"Then obey me!" roared Belknap savagely.

I was watching his gun. When it started to lift I thumbed back the hammer of my .44. It made an oily click-click that caused Belknap to stiffen and his gun stopped, sank back to rest on his thigh.

"You gave us orders, Colonel Belknap," said John quietly. "You like to give orders, don't you?"

Before Belknap could explode Overstreet said quickly, "Reverend, you better stop and think. There's an awful lot of innocent people in the line of fire. You wouldn't want to see any of them get hurt."

A gleam sparked from John's eyes and he spoke loud enough for the whole crowd to hear.

"Sir," he said, "are you threatening to shoot us down in cold blood if we don't obey Colonel Belknap's orders?"

Overstreet paled as he saw the trap he'd walked into. He protested, "No, now wait—"

"You mean," John overrode him, "that Belknap wants my brother and me killed so much he'd actually order his men to open fire on us—"

"But, I didn't—"

"—Knowing, *knowing,* sir, that some of the bullets would certainly rip into innocent men? would mangle the soft, tender flesh of their wives, the mothers of their children?" John's baritone boomed into a horrified demand:

"What kind of monster are you, sir? Is there no drop of compassion in your veins? Do you put your whims ahead of human decency?"

There was an ominous muttering from the ranch crowd behind us that alarmed even Belknap. Several of the Saber riders were starting to edge away. Overstreet took off his spectacles and polished them, his pale eyes darting here and there uneasily. He knew that a crowd could be a formless beast that nobody could control once it got out of hand, not even John.

Overstreet's slash of a mouth began to move as he muttered swiftly to Belknap. The Colonel looked like a man trying to swallow a mouthful of poison. His problem was that John spoke the truth. He did put his whims ahead of decency—and anything else. I had no doubt about it, Belknap would have gladly ordered his men to open up on us, and if a few of the ranch people got hit, all the better. It would teach them who was boss of Concho Basin. However, mad as Belknap was—and he was ready to spout fire and smoke out of his ears any minute—he had enough sense left to see that this wasn't the time to start trouble. It galled him almost beyond control to have to back down, but anything else had a good chance of ending with him getting lynched right there on the spot.

He couldn't just give up everything though. He swung his burning gaze to Blanche and he said thickly, "Well, at least we managed to save you, my dear. I—I hope the experience wasn't too dreadful, but we'll get you back to the doctor as quick as we can."

Even Overstreet's eyes bulged when he realized what

the Colonel was trying to put over. Sweat popped out on his forehead.

"For God's sake, Colonel," he whispered, "don't. Let her go, sir, there's plenty of—"

"Shut up," said Belknap. "Come along, Blanche, dear . . ."

He was starting to shove his black through to the Quincannon wagon when Blanche let out a shriek of terror and threw her arms around Mrs. Quincannon.

"No, no, don't let him touch me! Please! I hate him, I hate him! Don't let him take me away!"

I was so shocked I almost dropped my gun. By now I knew Blanche Maginnis well enough to expect almost anything from her, but one thing I didn't expect was to see her acting like a terrified female.

Whatever the reason it was enough to jar Belknap to a stop. He heard the sound of anger rising through the crowd and one glance around at their faces made him wheel the big stud and get back to his men fast. He stopped, turned to look back, nearly strangling on the emotions burning inside him.

"You . . . people," he suddenly shouted, "you listen to me! There's not going to be any election in Concho today. You hear? I swear this! So go home, you fools! You know you can't buck Saber! Go home or there'll be blood all over Concho Basin, and by God, it'll be your blood!"

Belknap brandished his saber high in the air so the early sunlight flashed redly on the blade, then he spun his stallion and led his riders off at a dead run.

He left behind him a real mixed-up mess, let me tell

you. Some of the people were all for going after him and stringing up him and his men to the nearest trees. A lot more wanted to turn their wagons around and go home.

A few cooler heads lined up with John to go ahead with the election the way they'd planned.

That sounds like a confusion that never would get straightened out, but there wasn't no real question about what they were all going to do. John had made sure of that with Mrs. Quincannon's help. It was why every man's wife was sitting beside him that day.

John had organized the women of the Basin. They had organized the election. There may have been men in that bunch who didn't want no part of electing a new sheriff, but if there were they weren't saying so out loud. This was women's day and their husbands were just going along to mark the ballots.

XXIX

THE WAGONS and hosses began moving again, and they every one were moving in the direction of Concho and the Lord only knew what kind of trouble. Belknap would be there and he'd have had the time to gather up all of his men and make preparations. I secretly wondered if there'd even be any town by the time we got there.

John must have guessed what I was thinking, the way he usually did, because he swung his hoss over close to mine and gave me a smile of encouragement. "Faith, brother," he said. "Faith."

When we finally came into sight of Concho and the place was still there I heard John chuckle softly to himself, then he started to sing:

> Now I tole de Lawd,
> I'se a sinner man,
> As bad as bad could be . . .

From the dusty cavalcade strung out behind us a hundred voices suddenly busted in to join him:

> But de Good Lawd said,
> Jest follow me,
> An' I will set yu free!

After that it was like we were going to a Fourth of July picnic or something, people singing and laughing all the way into town. Of course me and the Quincannon boys and a few others saw to it that our rifles were loaded and balanced across our pommels ready for action, but so far as we could see Belknap and Saber had gone home.

It didn't take long to find out that wasn't true, but for a fact the town was holding its own so far. Plastered across the front of the sheriff's office was a sheet with big black-painted letters on it, reading:

ELECTION TODAY!
VOTE HERE!

Guarding the polls was the darndest collection of

female women I ever hope to see. There were house-wives and the town blacksmith, Effie Peach, and a straight-up-and-down white-haired spinster that did the town sewing, and unless my eyes were going bad on me there were half a dozen saloon girls and a couple of painted-up females that were plain whores.

They were all dressed up fancy. Effie Peach was down-right unbelievable in candy pink with an enormous hat covered with purple flowers. Every time she moved I expected to see her bulging muscles bust a seam or some-thing. One thing the women had in common; they every one of them had some kind of weapon in their hands, from a sawed-off ten-gauge double-barreled shotgun in Effie's leathery mitts down to the little nickel-plated pistols car-ried by the two whores.

The ranchers poured into the office to vote while John cornered Effie with questions about Saber. She scowled and waved the shotgun.

"They're around the corner at the stable," she rumbled. "We've been expecting them to attack, but . . ." Effie shrugged her broad shoulders.

It wasn't till Jim Maginnis showed up at a run that we found out what was happening at the stable. The boy had shinnied up on the stable roof and listened to Belknap and his crew having a whale of a row. The Colonel was nearly crazy with rage at the way he and his power was being defied by first John and me, then Blanche and Doc Holly, and now by the ranchers and townspeople. It was too much for Belknap and he was talking and acting like a wild man, Jim said. Overstreet was doing his best to cool

Belknap down but his best wasn't good enough this time.

"Every time he starts talkin' sense to the Kurnel," Jim reported with a gap-toothed grin, "why, ol' Belknap jest starts cussin' and shoutin' fer him to shet his goddammed mouth—"

"Jim!"

The boy scowled at John and said, "I'm jest tellin' yu what he said, Reverend John. I ain't cussin' myself!"

John pressed his lips together sternly, eyes holding Jim's.

"Very well. Go on. What about the Saber crew?"

The boy shrugged and scuffed his feet. "I dunno, some of them seemed to think Overstreet was right, but some of them were fer the Kurnel."

John questioned him closely on that point, but all he could get Jim to say was that the crew was pretty evenly divided in the argument with maybe an edge going to Belknap, on account of him offering a big bonus to the men that stuck with him.

"What about the other boys?" asked John finally. "They all in place?"

"Shore," said Jim.

"They all know what to do?"

"Shore."

"All right, you better get back to the stable and see what's going on. But, Jim—"

The boy paused and looked back at John in question. "You be very careful."

Jim flashed his gap-toothed grin. "Shore!"

I watched the barefoot boy race down the street and disappear between two buildings. I was thinking to myself that John's strategy was a solidly good one. Using the women and all, I mean. Even the kind of men that formed most of the Saber crew wouldn't like the idea of using guns where women would get hurt. In the Territory a woman-killer had no friends. He couldn't even buy help. So bonus or not there was a chance that Belknap wouldn't be able to attack.

"Here, now! Here, now, you women break this up! Move along! Go home! What do you mean taking over my office like this?"

It was Tom Maple, badge, belly and all. His face was flushed with angry indignation. He strode up waving his arms and shouting, "You hear me? Go home where you belong! I'm the law in Concho, and by God you women can't—"

Effie Peach stepped forward and rammed the muzzle of her young cannon into Maple's bulging stomach. I caught my breath, half-expecting to see the round pot go pop like a balloon.

"We can't what?" asked Effie in a polite rasp.

Maple gulped, tried, gulped again, gasped, "Y-you, can't—" His squeak ended in a squawk as Effie nudged his belly again.

"You said that," she growled.

Maple tried to pull his stomach out of range. "Now, you listen to me—"

Effie nudged again. "We don't want to."

"B-but you've got to! I'm the sheriff of this county—"

"Were!" corrected Effie Peach. "We decided to elect us

a good one."

She reached over and lifted Maple's badge, taking half his vest along with it. He wailed in objection, which she didn't seem to hear. John stepped up to Maple then, pushing Effie's gun aside with a look of rebuke at the burly woman. John turned to Maple.

"Maple, for a smart man you're not using your brains," John said, wagging his head gravely. Maple eyed him uneasily, shifted from one foot to the other.

"You . . . what do you mean?"

"Well," sighed John sadly, "a smart man should be able to read the handwriting on the wall. You've been taking Belknap's pay for a long time now, but that's over with. Done for. Finished."

"F-finished?"

"Finished," agreed John.

Maple took a deep breath and managed a weak sneer. "You're dreaming."

"Am I? You'd better look around you."

Maple looked. "So?"

"So those are the people of this county. People who've had enough of Colonel Belknap's law, yes and Colonel Belknap, too!"

"Let 'em! They can't whip Belknap! He's the biggest man in the Territory!"

"You ought to read the Bible," said John. "There's a story about David and Goliath you'd find very interesting."

Maple looked around again, licked his lips nervously and patted his pot with shaky fingers. "Now, look here,

Reverend, you can be arrested for incitin' folks to riot—"

"But not for inciting them to vote," John interrupted. His voice went hard. "Don't be a fool, Maple. These people are electing a new sheriff today! Someone who'll see that justice is carried out in Concho. That means law-breakers like Colonel Belknap—and officials who betrayed the law—like you—are going to be punished for their crimes!"

"P-p-pun-pun—" Maple couldn't seem to get the word out. His face had taken on a greenish cast.

"Punished!" said John helpfully. "Yuma Penitentiary for a good many years—unless, of course, they decide not to wait for the circuit judge and hold a mass hanging."

Maple's knees started to buckle and he tried to swallow something that wouldn't go down. John added softly, "A wise man might think that this was a good time to go someplace far away. In a hurry." John paused. "What do you think?"

Maple showed what he thought by suddenly spinning around and making tracks down the street. When he reached his saddled hoss he hit the kak and spurred out of town like the devil was panting on his hind end. Maybe he was at that. One thing I was pretty sure about. Concho had seen the last of Mister Tom Maple.

John was going chuckle, chuckle to himself when he stopped real quick and moved to meet Jim, who was running up. The boy's face was as pale as it could get through eleventeen thousand freckles. He was chattering so fast the words came out bumping each other's heels but John got him slowed down enough so we could understand what he was saying.

What he said put the ice in my gut for sure. Belknap had stopped listening to Overstreet and had most of his men gathering chunks of pitch pine for torches.

"He's gunna burn down the hull town, Rev'rend John!" gasped Jim excitedly. "He said he was gunna burn everthin' clear down to ashes, an—"

I left John talking to the boy and headed down the street. On the way I picked up Brian O'Brian, who'd made the trip into Concho in the Quincannon's spare buckboard, sitting alongside Kate-Ellen. Brian was still favoring his bum leg but he could walk and when he saw the look on my face he hobbled over alongside me.

"What's up?" asked the big Irishman.

I told him about Belknap's plans for torching the town and pointed at the corner of the cross street that led to the livery stable.

"I figure that corner's a pretty good place to slow them down. You round up the Quincannons and the rest and set up a blockade across the street—"

I stopped because Brian was shaking his shaggy head stubbornly.

"Frank Niles," he said, "I've nivir in all my days seen a man so set on bein' a dead hero. I'll come with ye."

"You get that blockade set up!" I snarled.

"The ithers'll do that," the giant replied. "Ye need somebody to take care of ye, and the Rivirind John is busy right now."

"Wha-a-a-t? Take care of me?" I fumed. "Why, you big slab-sided peanut-brained mick, you know dammed well

189

that if it wasn't for me—"

"Don't be cursin'. Ye know the Rivirind does not like to hear ye talk like that."

Before I could slug him we were at the corner and had to duck for cover. Down the side street we could see that a big bonfire had been started in front of the livery stable, and Saber men were mounting and being handed lighted torches by a man tending the fire. Not all the Saber men; some were riding down the street out of town. Now a couple more tossed their torches back into the fire and rode to join them. But Belknap still had a healthy force of twenty-five or thirty men. Belknap, himself, was mounted on his black stallion. He was in the street waiting for his riders to equip themselves with torches. Overstreet was mounted, too, and was beside Belknap, arguing and yelling and making pleading gestures, all of which the Colonel ignored. Belknap sat his stud like a statue, coldly sure of himself. His decision was made.

Seeing that his men were ready Belknap gave a hand signal and led the way toward our corner. Overstreet stayed with him for a few last-ditch arguments. They got him nowhere. By that time he and Belknap were close enough for us to hear the last exchange between them.

Overstreet yanked his bay around in front of Belknap, forcing him to stop.

"All right," yelled Overstreet savagely. "All right. You want to commit suicide, go ahead! Go ahead! But not me, old man! Not me!"

Belknap kind of stiffened and said, "What did you call me?"

"I'll call you worse than that," shouted Overstreet. "You're a crazy old fool who's throwing away an empire all on account of you can't get that redheaded little slut out of your head! Well, I'm through! I'm through with Saber and I'm through with you!" He bowed mockingly. "Adios, Colonel Belknap!"

Spinning his bay on its hind feet Overstreet lashed him into a run down the street. He was heading out of town but he didn't get very far. Belknap jerked the carbine from his saddle holster, and leveling it, he drove shot after shot into Overstreet's back.

It was sheer butchery. With the first shot the Missouri gunman arched in the saddle and tried to turn, then the second and third slugs hit and drove him face down on his hoss's neck. He tried to hang on, but slowly slid from the saddle to sprawl in the dusty rutted street. He was dead when he hit but Belknap threw a last shot into him before lowering his rifle. He reloaded it calmly, gave his men a cold look and lifted his hand high.

"Let's go!" he cried sharply.

Belknap started off. Behind him the riders were looking back and forth at each other. They didn't like that cold-blooded killing of Overstreet, not even a little bit. Three or four of them turned their hosses and rode off, but most of the crew finally decided to follow Belknap.

I was lifting my rifle to take a good bead on the Colonel's third brass button when all of a sudden I felt two big arms scooping me off my feet and I was being carried away at a limping run.

"Hey, leggo!" I roared angrily. "Put me down! *Put me*

down, you goddammed big jackass!"

Brian had my arms pinned but I kicked and fought as best I could. He paid no attention, just kept pounding on up the street to where John and the Quincannons had set up a blockade of boxes and barrels.

Halfway there Brian saw he didn't have no chance to reach it before Belknap's bunch was turning the corner, so he lunged between two buildings and dumped me behind a big water barrel. Before I could get my feet under me Brian fell on top of me, holding me down with what felt like about a thousand pounds of solid beef.

"Quit it, now!" he panted. "Stop fightin', I'm only carryin' out John's orders!"

"John's ord—" I nearly strangled in my fury and fought all the harder to get loose. As soon as I got free I swore to myself that I'd take my brother and Brian and—

"Here they come!" gasped Brian.

I stopped fighting and stretched my neck to look around the water barrel, my head just underneath Brian's. I groaned wildly at what I saw. They were coming all right, heading up the street with Belknap out in front brandishing his saber. He waved it at some of his men as a signal for them to drop off and start torching the buildings on either side.

"Lemme go," I panted frantically. "At least let me get a shot at that brass-buttoned bastard before—"

Right then is when it happened again, almost exactly as it happened the night before. Saber hosses started blowing up, rearing and bucking and letting out piercing squeals of pain. They spun and twisted and kicked and climbed all over each other, tossing riders this way and that, acting like no hosses I'd ever seen act before.

Knowing what was happening and looking up I could see the tousled heads popping into sight over the edges of the roofs then ducking down again. The kids were up only long enough to let fly with their slingshots, then ducked down to reload. It being daylight I thought sure the Saber men would spot them and maybe they did, but if so they were too busy trying to stay in the saddle to do anything about it.

More than anything else the thing that drove those hosses absolutely nuts was all those flaming torches being slung around, a lot of them dropping into the street under their feet. Hoofs were kicking them, sending burning splinters every which way, and every time one of the coals landed on a hoss's hide the beast would do his dog-gonedest to corkscrew right up the side of the nearest building.

One big bearded rider was dumped on his hip pockets. Getting up, he spotted the source of all the trouble. Whipping out a gun he aimed and at the same time cut loose a bellow of warning.

"They're on the—"

Then a wild swinging torch caught him smack in the mouth. It dumped him on his butt again, sent his shot whistling off into the sky someplace, and set his beard to blazing. With an agonized howl he dropped his gun and clawed at his flaming beard, then headed for our water barrel at a dead run. Six feet away he dived headfirst in his frenzy to get his beard into the water. Brian reached up and when the man's head came up out of the water Brian's pistol barrel met it with a sodden thump. Water squirted from the man's mouth, then with a bubbly groan he curled up in front of the barrel and went to sleep.

I grabbed my chance and tried to squirm free. I made a few feet, then Brian's weight dropped back down on me with enough force to crack all my ribs.

"Stay put," he grumbled. "Ye're safe here."

Not having any wind left in my lungs I couldn't do any answering. Which was just as well, considering what I wanted to say.

On the street there wasn't nothin' left of Saber except hash. What riders could were getting out of there. At least ten men were lying around in the street, some of them out cold and a few of them trying to sit up, shaking their heads foggily and looking around for hosses that were about ninety miles from Concho or should have been the way they lit out.

The way fate does sometimes, Belknap was the only man still there and straddling a saddle. He was getting his stud under control, nearly breaking the black's neck doing it. He got a good look around him and started waving his saber and screaming like a fool woman. He hollered some of the awfullest language I ever heard come out of a man. It wasn't really cussing, I mean not real good clean man-type cussing. It was—well, it was—dirty! You know? Dirty and kind of wild and crazy-like, not making any real sense even.

He was almost foaming at the mouth like a mad dog by the time he ran out of words. Then all of a sudden he shook his saber and tried to force his panicky stallion to move over close enough so he could pick up one of the fallen torches. The stud was plumb against the idea and kept dancing and shuffling around and backing away. Belknap finally started to swing down to get the torch, but just as he took one foot from the stirrup the stud backed right over one of them torches and his long tail flared up with a whoosh.

I mean to say right here and now that no hoss at no time never ever came apart like that big stallion did right then. I tell you for true I thought he never would come down the way he jumped. He must have flung Belknap about ninety-five feet and the way the Colonel came whomping down in the middle of that street you tell he wasn't going to be up and doing for a month of Sundays, if at all.

The stud did his best to go six ways at the same time, then finally gave it up, and the last I seen of him the poor beast was leaving Concho, hitting the ground about every fifty yards or so with that beautiful tail of his nothing but a smoking stub. It gave me the miseries just thinking of the poor fellow that tried to ride that stud next. I mean, you could see that he was one hoss that had lost all his faith in people.

About then was when the laughing started, and pretty soon it sounded like everybody in Concho Basin was haw-hawing their fool heads off all at once. I thought back to what Blanche had said the night before and had to agree with her. Colonel Rye W. Belknap had stopped being a boogeyman. Folks would never be able to feel scared of him again, they'd be laughing too hard.

Brian finally let me loose and while I was trying to make up my mind which I'd go after first, him or John, I saw that John had enough trouble for the moment. He was standing straddle of Belknap and holding off two mad-faced females, both of who were waving guns and yelling at John and trying to move around to get a clear shot at the unconscious Colonel.

Me and Brian ran over and each grabbed one of the women and held them as best we could while John took their guns away.

"Lemme go, you big ape," shrieked the Scotch one, kicking Brian's shins.

"I'm going to shoot that devil's head off!" yelled Blanche.

"You are not!" yelled Mrs. Quincannon. "I am!"

"Like hell! I am!"

That's when John roared, *"Shut up!"*

The women stopped struggling and kicking and stared at him like he'd just grown another head or something. John put his Look on Blanche. "And you stop that cursing, Blanche Maginnis!"

Believe it or not, all Blanche said back was "Yes, John."

John looked at them steadily for a moment.

"Ladies," he said finally, only it came out like a dirty word. He went on acidly, "Good, respectable, Christian ladies. Fighting in public to see who gets the chance to murder a man in cold blood!"

"Aw, now, John, wait," I busted in. "They—"

"Shut up," he said. Still looking at the women, he went on: "Both of you mothers, with children that expect you to set them an example. Well, I tell you right now—you make me sick!"

"That's not fair, John!" cried Blanche.

"Fair? Fair? Since when are you two looking for fairness? You're after blood! Vengeance! Death!"

"He caused the death of my husband—" said Mrs. Quincannon grimly.

"Mine, too!" snapped Blanche.

John made a savage gesture of disgust.

"Very well. You want to be just like him, you want to play God and executioner. All right."

John took a pistol from his belt and handed it to Blanche. It was his gun, not one of theirs. "Go ahead," he said. "Kill him if that's what you want."

Me and Brian both started protesting but John shut us up with a look and continued, "Go on, kill him. I'm not going to force you to obey the law or God. So go ahead, get it over with, but—have the decency to stop calling yourself a Christian, please."

Blanche held the gun in both hands, pointing it at Belknap, wanting to shoot so bad she could taste it. Then she started to tremble and she shook her head violently. She shoved the gun back at John, muttering, "No. No. I can't do it," then ran off.

John took the gun and handed it to Mrs. Quincannon, who stared at it like she'd never seen a gun before; then with a shudder she threw it to the ground and started to cry softly. Brian put his arm around her shoulder.

"Go ahead and cry, Ma," he said gently. "It's all right."

It wasn't till he'd led her away that I realized what he'd

called her. I started to say something to John but saw the smile on his face and knew he'd heard. I shook my head a little.

"Well, you got away with it," I said. "But do you mind telling me how you knew they wouldn't just go ahead and plug him?"

John gave me a smile. "Faith, brother," he murmured. "Faith."

He moved off. I bent over and picked up the gun Mrs. Quincannon had thrown down. I looked at it and found out that as usual John hadn't left everything up to God. There wasn't a single bullet in that gun.

Effie Peach went over to hand Mrs. Quincannon the badge she'd lifted from Tom Maple, but Mrs. Quincannon shook her head and gave it to Duncan.

"Duncan's The Quincannon, now," she said. "He better wear this. I've got too much work to do at home."

Ten minutes after Duncan and the others had dragged Belknap and what was left of his crew into the jail, Lt. Kermit Ogilvy rode into Concho at the head of two troops of the Sixth Cavalry. He had a warrant for Belknap and Overstreet on the charges of murder and defrauding the U.S. government.

When we turned over the prisoners to him, one live and one dead, the hard-bitten lieutenant couldn't resist a puzzled question as to how a handful of citizens had accomplished what he'd brought half a squadron of cavalry to do.

I glanced down the street at John and Ben Steiner laughing and handing out bags of candy to a bunch of kids that had slingshots sticking out of their hip pockets. I shook my head.

"Don't ask, Lieutenant. Even if I told you, you'd never believe it."

X X X

I WATCHED JOHN saddling up with a funny hollow kind of feeling inside me. I don't know why. I'd certainly live a lot longer not riding with him. I'd be free to cuss and have a drink and well, do lots of things that he was always nagging me about. I should have felt happy.

But I didn't, I felt miserable. It didn't help a bit to have him being so cheerful and all, either. He was humming and singing to himself as he packed up; and now as he mounted, he gave me a big warm smile and put his hand on my shoulder.

"Be good, Frank," he said. "I'll miss you, and I'll pray real hard for you to win the victory over that cursing habit."

Just then Blanche Maginnis and Jim rode up with a pack hoss trailing after them. Blanche smiled at John.

"Ready, John?"

He nodded. "All ready." He lifted his hand to me. "So long, Frank."

Blanche and Jim gave me waves and the three of them were gone, trotting their hosses down the trail together. I gaped after them like a fool, then yelled, "Hey, wait, where's *she* going?"

John called back, "She's my new organizer! She's going to do my advance work for me!"

"But . . . but . . . she can't!" I bellowed. "What about the boy's schooling? She can't go on your circuit!"

"John and I will teach him," came Blanche's voice faintly.

"But . . . but . . . wait! Come back! That's crazy! You can't do this to me! Come back!"

I ran after them, yelling my fool head off. Then I suddenly skidded to a halt and looked back at Slug who was saddled and tied to the corral rail. I legged it back fast and with a flying mount I took off after John and his new organizer. I dug the hooks into Slug. I knew what I was letting myself in for, but somehow I didn't care. After all, like my ma said, somebody had to look after my brother, John.

"Hey! Wait for me!"

Center Point Publishing
600 Brooks Road • PO Box 1
Thorndike ME 04986-0001 USA

(207) 568-3717

US & Canada:
1 800 929-9108